Liminal: Astro Mining Enterprises.

Q.R.Kode

Published by Q.R.Kode, 2024.

LIMINAL: ASTRO MINING ENTERPRISES.

First edition. December 19, 2024.

ISBN: 979-8230626800

Written by Q.R.Kode.

LIMINAL:
ASTRO MINING ENTERPRISES!

How would I describe our adventures?
The places we went? The people we met? The stories we shared? Well...
It all began on a world most would call unremarkable, except for 3
friends. With their boundless adventure across the little blue jewel
they inspired many... Sadly, all adventures must come to an end sooner
or later... Or do they?

Prologue.
A soft chill blew through the city. Pieces of litter and rubbish tumbled
along the streets and alleyways. A sight most everyone ignored, except
for a pair light-Hazel eyes watching from the balcony of a rooftop
diner.
A young man sat near the balcony railing, watching the city below
slowly fade into the night. Traffic died out as lights across the city
went dark. Soon, the only sound he heard was the soft whipping of the
wind, and his own thoughts. He stared at the cup of coffee in his
hands as the wind carried the steam away.
After a moment he sighed and placed the cup on the table, then
walked over to the railing. He placed his knees against a lower rail and
leaned over the top rail with his arms spread.
Tears rolled down his cheek as he held a soft smile.
"I'm gonna miss this planet." He said with a subtle pride.
He then leaned over the edge further as his boots lost grip on the
damp gravel. As his weight shifted over the railing something caught
the neck of his coat and yanked him backwards, accompanied by the
voice of an angry young woman.
"JACEN YOU SON OF A BITCH!"

He tumbled along the rooftop. As he came to a stop, a metallic claw lifted him up and wrapped him tightly in a warm metal tendril in front of a pair Red digital eyes.

"So you're just gonna leave without saying goodbye!?" A shrill, electronic female scolded.

"Trixie! Ashlynn!" Jacen gasped. "I'm sorry."

Ash walked over beside Trixie and they both scowled at him. Before him, Jace could Ash standing with her arms crossed. Her coat rustled with the breeze as the beanie on her head draped lightly. Next to her was a cybernetic 4-wheeler with a large metal tail protruding from under her frame, still squeezing him tight. In place of headlights were 2 pixelated Red eyes, staring at him with intensity.

"Not even a call?" Trixie asked with a sad anger.

"Trixie I'm sorry, okay?" Jacen gasped again. "I don't know what I was thinking."

"You never do, Jace." Ashlynn scoffed with a sigh. "Put him down Trix." Trixie lowered him the roof and unraveled her arm, giving him a soft but meaningful slap across the face as she pull her claw away.

As he rubbed his cheek, Jace looked back over to the railing then back to Ash with tears in his eyes.

"Y-you saved my life." He sighed. "You know that?"

"Funny." Ashlynn smirked. "You always do something and we end up saving your life."

"What time does your ship leave?" Trixie asked.

As Jace looked toward her, he noticed her eyes were back to their bright Green color.

"How did you..."

"You left a note, dumbass." Ash and Trixie interrupted in unison. They smirked at eachother then looked back to Jace.

"Hop on." Trixie invited softly. "We wouldn't want you to miss."

A short while later, Trixie came racing out of the shipping alley with Ash corraling Jace as they both held gripped the handlebars.

The wind rustled their hair and rippled their faces as Trixie rocketed across the city on empty streets.

Sometime later, the trio came drifting into the parking lot and screeching to a halt near the terminal bar.

Jacen collapsed off his 4-wheeled friend and slumped on the cold ground below, struggling to catch his breath.

"Do you...always...have to...do that..., Trixie?!"

Ash giggled as she composed herself.

"Heh..., you won't last long out there if you collapse after a rocket ride!"

Trixie chuckled along with her as she helped Jacen off the ground and limped him over to an open table.

Round after round, hour after hour, they drank and laughed and cried and remembered their time together, until they noticed the time.

"Oh shyett!" Trixie slurred. "Yerr goin ta bee late!"

Still sobering up, Jacen lurched from his chair and fell to the morning ground, before being hoisted up by Ash.

"You ain't that drunk, star surfer." She taunted. "Let's get you going."

As he struggled to keep his footing, he fell into Ash with a hug and cried softly.

"Ash, Trixie..., I'm sorry, okay?! I'm gonna miss you both, I'm sorry I didn't tell you..."

"It's okay." Ash interrupted with a sad giggle. "We..., We would have done the same!"

"You guys aren't mad?" He choked softly.

"No we're pissed." Trixie giggled drunkenly.

"But..." Ash continued. "You went through all this trouble, no point in turning back now."

He hugged Ash tighter, burying his face into her shoulder.

"Jacen." She sighed. "You can't hang on forever."

"Yes I can." He cried softly. "Don't tempt me."

"Don't forget genius." Trixie added softly. "If you stay, we'll be here with ya."

Jacen looked down at her, who gave him a devious, somewhat threatening wink.

He gave in, pulling Ash closer as Trixie wrapped her tendril around them both, lifting them off the ground.

After a few tear filled moments, she set them down and rolled back.

"let's get you going." Ash assured him.

They talked as they made their way through the terminal building.

"Why don't you guys come with me?" Jacen asked.

Trixie and Ash giggled heartily.

"We would love to Jace." Trixie began.

"But you know us." Ash continued. "We would end up destroying a planet or something."

They all chuckled softly as they approached the final checkpoint.

" Oh shit!" Ash exclaimed. "Almost forgot."

Jacen watched curiously as she pulled a glowing wristband from her pocket. He could see pulsating blue circuitry that danced around the band like water.

"What it is?" He asked, grabbing it softly.

"Trix and I made it." Ash continued. "We were going to give it to you on our next adventure. A gift for our friendship anniversary."

"Ash." He said with misty eyes. "Thank you."

She and Trixie gave in one last time and embraced him in a tight hug.

"You can't hold on forever." He playfully mocked them.

"Smartass!" They replied in unison.

After setting them down again, Jace walked away, stubbornly holding back tears.

"One more thing!" Ash said, pacing after him.

Grabbing the wristband, She held it up near a light.

"It's also an emergency beacon." She began. "Just incase you decide to have fun without us!"

Jace sniffled.
"If you ever get into trouble, you better use it!"
She teased.
"Or there'll be trouble!" Trixie added.
"I will." He said. "Promise."
They shared one last quick hug.
"We're gonna miss you Jace." Ashlynn sniffled.
"Keep in touch, alright?" Trixie added.
"I will." Jacen replied, stepping through the checkpoint.

Chapter 1

Jacen was surrounded by a thick, inky blackness. The smell of aged mold and stale air lingered about.

"H-hello?" He called out.

His voice echoed and reverberated as gaslamps began to appear on the walls before him, revealing a brick and mortor hallway, the kind from the ancient days of steampower. Alone, Jace stepped quietly down the hall, until he arrived at the entry way to a massive train platform. Like raoming spirits, the gaslamps continued fading onto the pillars before him. Jacen curiously followed the lamps along the stone pillars into the darkness, across iron and stone bridges that arched over massive pairs of rails and under cautiously hanging signs written in weird languages, looking back every so often to make sure there was still a path behind him.

For what seemed like several lifetimes, he wondered, until he noticed light eminating from opposite side of the cavernous room.

"Ash?" He gasped.

She stood on edge of the darkened platform, illuminated from underneath by a pair of glowing rails. She appeared to be talking with someone, a shadowy shilluette it seemed. Excitedly, Jacen sprinted over the remaining bridges, outpacing the lamps. As he neared the final bridge, the sound of horns, bells and whistles exploded out from the last tunnel. Painful and deafening, Jace had to cover his ears tight to remain concious. As he stepped and stumbled over the last bridge, A cloud of glowing, golden steam flooded out of the tunnel and filled the open section of the tracks. Held in place by somekind of barrier, the steam pulsed and danced and sparkled, quickly fading to reveal a giant luminescent train.

As Ashlynn grabbed her bags and walked over to the doors, Jacen took off running! Every step seemed to bring him no closer, until the door hissed shut. Like a bolt of lightining, Jacen shot across the expansive platform!

"ASH, DON'T GO!" He cried out.

Ash took a seat by the window and placed a hand on it with tears in her eyes, She was looking right at him. As the train lurched forward, Jace veered parallel as it picked up speed.

With the opposite wall approaching, Jace pumped his legs as fast as he could, trying to place his hand on the window, trying to match her gesture, but the train kept inching ahead.

"NO!"

With a cry of pain, his knee popped and he tumbled along the floor as the train dissapeared into the opposite tunnel, the ambient glow and warm steam following it.

"ASH NO, PLEASE!" He wept. "I'M SORRY, PLEASE COME BACK!"

He cried bitterly as the room fell dark, illuminated by the gaslamps he previously out ran. As they formed a circle on the pillers nearby, Jacen instinctively moved into the light as the lamps he followed were now gone.

Alone, he wept in the circle of dim light, until there was a tap on his shoulder.

Looking up, Jace could see a dark skinned girl with glowing Orange hair. As she knelt down, he saw a pair of Amber eyes, and a sad smile. The girl hoisted him up, and brushed his shoulders. He thought for a moment, his pain was gone. With a soft giggle she pulled a small box from behind her back, it was Onyx, wrapped with a pulsing Yellow bow.

"Here. " She cooed. "She wanted you to have this."

Jace cautiously took the box from her hands, silently running his eyes over it.

"You'll see them again." She assured him. "And many more like them."

Her words sent a frigid chill along his spine, as Jace looked up to respond, the girl had already begun fading into inky Blackness outside the pillars.

"It was nice to finally meet you..., Jacen."

The words echoed around him faintly as she became no more.

After a moment of frantic searching, Jacen brought his attention back to the box. It was lighter than it looked, and smoother than it appeared.

Cautiously, and slowly, He undid the ribbon and bow, and lifted the top off as it let out a faint hiss. Inside the gift box was a glowing 3 sided pyramid. After he pulled it out, the box faded and the pyramid began shifting colors. From Blue, to Red, to Yellow, It cycled through more and more colors, getting faster with each one, until it was glowing solid White.

It grew brighter and hotter, as the gaslamps faded, leaving only him. Jace wanted to drop it, but something told him not to. Within seconds he was blinded with a painful brightness as searing heat burned his hands.

He woke up with a violent jolt.

Gasping and Wheezing, and drenched in a cold sweat, he frantically checked around the room, then over to the projected wall-clock.

With a heavy sigh, he moved off the bed and prepared his belongings as the ship began to dock.

After a quick rinse and a change of clothes, Jace made his way down to the ship's exit hall. Dock security scanned him and his bags, then sent him on his way.

As Jacen walked out from the entrance corridor, His eyes lit up in excitement! The space-port danced with life as travelers shifted about. Transit shuttles flew threw the air above the concourse, as hover cars and freight haulers flew beneath. At the far end of the massive atrium, a shipping port bustled with workers, on the other end, the entrance to the city sparkled as vehicles raced in and out of the tunnels beneath him.

With a deep breath, Jace looked over the center railing, admiring the artery of vehicles below, before continuing deeper in to the lively crowd of people.

After a short while, Jacen stopped to take a breath at the schedule board, and look for the next trolley time.

"Damnit." He thought. "Nothing for the next hour."

He found a bench nearby and took a well needed seat.

As Jacen relaxed, he failed to notice a cloaked thief making off with his bags, until the sound of his luggage dropping to the floor caught his attention.

"THIEF!" Jace cried. "STOP THEM!"

Chapter 2

Sweating heavily, Jacen barely managed to stay on the tail of the thief and his bags. As the thief ran into a dense crowd of travellers, a metal arm sprung out and caught the thief at the neck, sending him to the floor gasping for air.

As Jace caught up, and caught his breath, a tall lanky girl stepped over the hazbin thief and hoisted him up by the neck of his jacket. With an angry grunt she tossed him along the walkway and let off a deep, throaty chuckle.

As Jace stepped over to his bags, she turned around and gave him a view he never would've asked for.

On the end of her Left leg was a metal boot connected to a piston where her ankle and foot should be, on the end of her Right leg was a boot stained with dry blood. As he looked higher he noticed the metal stopped at her knee, moving upward he noticed she wore a patchy skirt that was torn across the crotch, revealing a pair of White bow-tie panties. Continuing upward he saw a fit, toned stomach covered in faded scars and scratches, above that was a chest wrap, covering what looked like a small pair of breasts, the wrap was covered with an open, sleeveless vest, also stained with blood. Her right arm was covered with several tattoos along with more scars and scratches, her left arm, the arm that saved his belongings, was metallic from her shoulder downward. Between her shoulders was a throbbing, scar covered neck, topped with a head sporting an angular face, a devilish, toothy grin, a Green Left eye and a patch covered Right eye.

She looked down at him with palpable malicious intent.

"Enjoyin the view?" She asked with a thick, menacing accent.

Jacen quickly picked himself and averted his gaze.

"I, uh...," Jace cleared his throat. "Thank you!"

"No worries Mr. Ahd." She replied. "But I would like to ask a favor of ya."

"Oh, yeah sure..." He paused. "How do you know my..."

"Luggage tag, dummy!" She interrupted. "Look I'm starving! Ya think ya could reward me with a bite to eat?"

He looked her in the eye and swollowed hard.

"I..., Sure."

"Awesome!" She replied happily. "There's a new restruant just down the way and I've been dying to try it out!"

Without another word she took each of his bags under an arm and started walking.

He stood to process what just happened before she called out.

"Hurry up I'm hungry!"

After a pricey meal, the girl finished her drink with an obnoxious burp, and stood up to leave as Jace began to motion.

"Name's Polly, we'll meet again don't worry."

As she walked out of the restruant she called out one last time.

"Try keeping your eyes open from now on! Dumbass!"

As Polly walked away, his heart dropped along with his eyes. The way her tattered skirt bounced along with her shaggy Brown hair gave him conflicting emotions.

After finishing his meal, Jacen tightly gripped his bags and walked out shortly after.

A short while later, an information pillar caught his eye.

Dozens of holographic screens orbited around the monolith, showing bits and pieces of the city; A shopping district filled with cute alien women, a sport stadium packed with roaring fans, and a public gathering to watch some kids have a dance off.

After checking the time on one of the screens, he looked around with a sigh, before noticing a pottery shop near by. The shop keeper greeted Jace with a wide, toothy smile.

"Lev begs harr, pless." The shopkeeper commanded softly.

"Look sir." Jace began. "I just..."

The shopkeeper pounded his fist on the counter as all four of his Purple eyes focused on Jacen.

Jace quickly rolled his bags to the counter and set them just in front of the counter, after which the shopkeeper relaxed.

As he walked along the center isle, he saw many strange alien designs lining the shelves. He glanced aimlessly, when something caught his eye; A small black urn, with blue circutry pulsing all around it. Jacen thought for a second, then looked at the wristband Ash had gifted him.

He noticed the circuitry on his wristband was pulsing in the exact same fashion.

Jacen curiously brought his wristband up to the urn to compare them. The circuitry had formed two circles; one on the urn, and one on the wristband. As he brought them closer the circles pulsed faster and faster, Jace could feel the air growing thicker around the wristband. Evermore curious, he brought them into contact with eachother. Just as they began to touch a bright arc of Blue energy shot to the wristband and up Jace's arm, sending him across the store and tumbling up to the window, almost breaking it.

The shopkeeper jumped the counter, revealing 4 muscular arms and 2 very stalky legs. He grabbed Jacen and his bags and tossed them out of the store before shouting.

"YEH NAT VOLCOME HARR!"

The shopkeeper watched as he picked himself and bags up, and quickly paced away from the store.

Just down the walkway, Jacen stopped to examine his arm. He couldn't see any damage, but there was a tingle. After testing his motor functions, he passed it off as a momentary shock and continued onward.

A short while later, he came across another schedule board, as a trolley pulled up along the rail.

As he ran to catch it, the wristband began to vibrate wildly. Jace was tempted to check it, but thought otherwise.

"No time!" He muttered, almost out of breath.

The seats were packed, but Jace managed to find standing space near the middle. As the trolley continued onward, He watched the holographic banner across the isle to pass time. Curious, he checked the wristband. The colors and patterns had settled into a slow, rythmic shift as they moved along. Jace then noticed the banner glitching and flickering wildly, as the words became clusters of strange and unknown symbols.

Sometime later, His stop came into view. He stepped out and quickly located his pickup; a young woman in a chauffer uniform, standing next to a limo with a sign. She had an auburn ponytail hanging from the chauffer's cap and a lock of hair obscuring her Left eye, leaving her Right eye to watch intensely with a Green stare, as he came towards the vehicle.

"Mr. Ahd?" She asked.

"Yes ma'am." Jace replied.

"This way please." She directed.

Minutes later they were hovering away.

"Strahp in please, Mr.Ahd." She warned coldly.

Her warning disturbed Jace, the way her accented voice carried the words.

As they flew higher into the city, He noticed the lines on the wristband shifting again. Bending and rotating, until they came to a stop in the shape of a single word.

"Hello."

Chapter 3

"Excited, Mr. Ahd?" The driver asked.

"For what?" He replied.

"To start working for us." She said assuringly.

"Oh, Yeah. Of course." He chuckled.

Jace checked the wristband again, failing to notice all the hover traffic slowing to a crawl.

"SHIT, HANG ON!" The driver yelled.

By the time he heard her, it was too late. She had already dropped out of the lane, nose-diving lower into the city! Jacen was pinned to his seat as the limo rocketed downward.

"WHAT THE HELL IS HAPPENING?" He shouted.

"SHUT UP AND TRUST ME, NOW STRAP IN!" The driver shouted back.

As the vehicle leveled out near the ground Jace bounced out of the seat onto the floor. As he climbed back onto the leathery bench and strapped himself in, he glanced out the back window as fear shot along his spine.

A missle was coming straight at him.

"OKAY, I TRUST YOU!" He cried. "NOW PLEASE GET US OUT OF HERE!"

As it grew closer, Jace prayed, hoping the driver knew what she was doing. He was sucked into the seat again as they banked around a corner. Barely catching them, the missle was sent into a building as they cut another turn. By the time it detonated, they were already out of range.

Bullets started bouncing off the trunk as they weaved up and around skyskrapers.

"LOOK!" Jace cried. "I KNOW I DID SOMETHINGS IN THE PAST..."

"HOLD TIGHT!" The driver interupted.

Jacen was sucked into the seat once more as the driver ignited the rocket boosters, launching them higher into the clouds. He watched silently as they fell behind.

"They'll just be waiting for us." He said.

"Then let's keep them waiting!" She replied.

As the limo sped torwards the sky-barrier, another missile came flying at them from the side.

"SHIT!" The driver cried.

As she rolled and banked the vehicle, Jace bashed his head against the window and blacked out, accidently hitting the S.O.S button, as he collapsed to the floor.

The limo danced up through the clouds as it evaded the missle, while Jacen's wristband began to pulsate wildly and vibrantly as the circuitry began forming words.

In a strange manuver, the driver pointed the limo back toward the city and began diving rapidly. The missle got closer and closer as they neared the riverfront district. As they were about to hit the water, the driver banked the vehicle upwards and ignited the boosters again, Barely avoiding the missle as it impacted the river and exploded into a cloud of steam.

Gaining altitude again, the driver put the vehicle at full speed as they rocketed upwards toward the barrier once more. With the push of a button, arcs of electricity shot from the limo as they neared the barrier. With the press of another button, the vehicle made itself airtight as they shot through the ionized barrier, and out into open space.

After a few minutes, the vehicle stopped shaking as they exited the planet's gravity field. With a sigh of relief, the driver undid her restraints and took a breath. After a few moments, she relaxed herself and spoke softly.

"Mr. Ahd I realize this has been quite a shock and is in need of proper explanation, so I'll keep it simple. Jacen Ahd, you are..."

She paused.

Curious, she looked into the rear of the limosine, and saw Jacen collapsed on the seat with blood dripping from the side of his head.

"AW SHIT!" She exclaimed.

After fetching a med-kit from the passenger seat she made her to the back of the limo, where she noticed a small bloodstain on the window.

"Mordis is gonna kill me!" She whimpered.

After wrapping Jacen's skull she checked his pulse with a relieved sigh, then made her back to the driver seat and strapped her self in.

Entirely unnoticed, Jacen's wristband softly eminated light as it now displayed more words.

"NEED HELP!"

Chapter 4

Ashlynn sat with her legs over the edge, watching the sun drop below the horizon. Trixie sat next to her, flicking pebbles into the ocean beneath them. With a sigh, Ash pulled a small cube from her bag and tapped it a few times. A holographic screen flickered open, revealing a picture.

The picture showed a younger Jace and Ash, sitting on Trixie. They were all smiling, holding up V-fingers. With teary eyes, She held the cube to her chest, with memories running through her head.

"Miss you buddy." She sighed.

"You could have stopped him ya know." Trixie spoke softly. "Why didn't you?"

"Why didn't you?" Ash mocked lightly.

The electronic 4-wheeler grumbled for a moment, then let off a sigh.

"Do I have to answer?"

"Messin with ya, Trix." Ash replied.

As the dropped lower, Ash grabbed her things and scooted closer to Trixie, resting on her as they watched the day end.

"Hey Trix?" Ash wondered.

"Yeah?" She answered softly.

"It's been a few years, hasn't it?" Ash continued.

"Since what?" Trixie asked.

"Since you spoke with your..."

She was interrupted as her communicator beeped. Grabbing it from her pack, she examined it closely.

"What the...?"

Ash went silent for a moment, looking over the device.

"What?" Trixie replied. "What is it?"

"I just got some garbled messages." Ash wondered softly.

"Oh!" Trixie squeaked. "Is it from..."

"OH FUCK!" Ashlynn exclaimed.

"What?" Trixie worried. "Ash what?!"

Ash hurriedly collected her things as she replied.

"One reads "Hello"...,"

Trixie began to speak.

"Okay, so..."

"And the other one says "NEED HELP!""

Trixie remained silent as Ashlynn climbed on her saddle.

"Trixie it's from the wristband, I think Jace is in trouble, WE NEED TO GO NOW!"

As soon as Ash gripped her handlebars, Trixie shot away from the cliff and back towards the city. A trail of dirt and dust followed them closely.

The sun finished dropping below the horizon as Trixie raced herself into the night-time city.

"TRIXIE COME ON!" Ash yelled. "WE GOTTA HURRY!"

Trixie cackled joyfully as they started up a hill outside the city. Both screeched excitedly as they came flying over the barrier wall, and down into the path of a speed checker.

Several patrol cruisers began following them as they entered the city expressway. As the lights strobed behind them, Trixie pulled ahead.

"Trixie, evasive manuevers!" Ash commanded.

"Who do you think you're riding, Genius!" She quipped.

As they came up a secondary on-ramp, Trixie rode up along the guard-wall and rotated herself as she flew over the median. Landing in the opposite lane, the cybernetic quadbike flattened herself to the ground as she raced under oncoming traffic. Ash pressed herself against the excited chassis as tight as she could while vehicles rocketed above them.

A short while later, an entrance ramp came into view.

"TAKE THAT EXIT!" Ash yelled.

Trixie cackled again.

"I THINK YOU MEAN..."

"JUST GO!" Ashlynn screamed.

As soon as she could, Trixie launched herself off the road and onto the inner guard-wall before launching herself again onto the outer guard-wall. As they picked up speed on the way down, Ashlynn shouted worriedly.

"TRY NOT TO KILL US TRIXIE!"

"NO PROMISES!" She taunted.

As they came out of the ramp tunnel, Trixie launched herself once more, clearing both lanes entirely they went from one tunnel to the other. As they came drifting out into the proper lane, Trixie ignited her boosters as they slid around the intersection.

After sometime, they came sliding onto the front lawn of their bungalo as Ashlynn jumped onto the grass and kicked the door in.

"START PACKING!" She yelled. "I'LL GET THE SHIP READY!"

She ran up to a control terminal and began entering commands, when the memory that night hit her. Ash stood motionless, as worry began to fill her mind. After a moment of silence, tears began rolling down her cheek.

"ASH?" Trixie exclaimed, rolling up behind her.

She softly choked back tears as a metal claw rested on her shoulder.

"He'll be okay, Ash." Trixie reassured. "Come on, Patrol will be here soon."

"Yeah." She answered quietly. "Good call Trix. You got everything?"

"Everything!" Trixie replied confidently.

She lowered her tail into the crate and pulled out a cluster of weapons and a small sack.

"Good." Ash sighed. "Let's get going."

After she entered the final command, the floor rotated open, revealing the nose-cone of a patchwork ship. As it rose from the floor, they stepped back. The roof creaked and slid open, revealing a dark, star filled sky.

They stood quietly for a moment.

"Beautiful." Trixie said.

"Yeah." Ash replied. "It's been a while."

"Didn't think we'd be here this long." Trixie quipped.

Ash sighed heavy.

"Neither did I."

They remained silent as they looked into the sky.

"Once a star pirate..." Trixie began.

"...always a star pirate." Ash finished. "Time to go home."

As their hoverpad came to a stop, the entry door slid open with a hiss. Making themselves comfy, Ash reached into her bag, pulled out the cube and tapped it again. After one last look at the picture, she pulled open a layer of her chest wrap and secured the cube inside.

"Ready?" She asked.

"Never was, never will be." Trixie sighed.

"Me neither." Ash replied, igniting the engines.

Chapter 5

Jace woke up in a daze, The room around him spun wildly as his eyes adjusted. When it finally stopped he found himself in a medical observation room, with a pounding headache. As he sat up to rub his head, arm and chest retraints held him down.

"Hello?" He called out frantically.

"Hello." A voice replied coldly.

Jace let out a sigh of relief.

"Mind letting me out of..."

"Yes." The voice interupted. "I do mind. I'll let you out, but I want some answers first!"

"Answers for what?" He asked worriedly.

The voiced sighed in frustration.

"Look." He said. "If I said I had no Idea, would you believe me?"

"No, not really, no." The voice replied.

He remained silent.

"First things first." The voice continued. "What do you know of the attacks?"

"Attacks?" Jace replied worriedly.

"You've got to be shitting me!" The voice sighed.

He noticed the voice sounded very familiar.

"Hey!" He said. "You're my driver."

"You got it." She replied sarcastically, clicking her tongue.

Within seconds he could feel the straps release. As Jacen sat up in the bed, he was greeted with by a familiar face. She sat near the the foor of the bed, looking over a file folder.

"Feel free to stretch, Jacen" She said.

As he slid off the bed, the driver stood up to greet him.
He was able to get a better look at her. Before him stood the same girl from before, but something was different. She had soft yet pronounced facial features, and a look that meant business. They locked eyes as she extended her hand, and that's when he saw it.
Hidden under the Auburn lock of hair, was a Blue eye.
"Chief Officer of Intelligence. Miranda Rachel Briggswelle, at your service, Mr. Ahd." She said, twirling her other hand.
"Uh, Jace," He replied. "Jacen Thaddeus Ahd. How do you know my..."
"As an undercover agent," Miranda interupted. "I had to know everything about my "target". That's you."
He stood confused, gazing into her heterchromic eyes.
"Target for what?" He asked.
"You're kidding me." Miranda replied.
"I'm not?" Jacen answered cautiously.
"Interrogations are gonna have fun with you." She said, looking at the file.
"INTERROGATIONS?" He worried. "FOR WHAT?"
Miranda rubbed the bridge of her nose in frustration.
"Because you're under arrest, dipshit!"
"What? Why?" He whined. "I'm innocent."
"I'm sure you are." She mocked. "Now please follow me."
As Miranda looked back at the file, Jacen's head began pounding again. As he reached for his temples, he remembered his wristband. As Miranda continued looking over the files, he pressed the emergency button.
Unbeknownst to Jacen, the officer caught his motion in the corner of her eye. As she took a breath to speak, a man in a captain's uniform quietly stepped in.
"BRIGGSWELLE!" He commanded angrily.
"YES CAPTAIN!" Miranda shouted, almost dropping the file.
"WHAT THE HELL IS GOING ON?!" The captain replied.

Chapter 6

The patchwork vessel shot through space like a bullet, racing through planetary bodies. The engines hummed quietly as the star-bound duo kept watch from their seats."What's our E.T.A?" Trixie sighed in defeat.

"How long?" Trixie asked.

"We're at full power!" Ash replied. "10 minutes."

Several moments later, they began to notice patrol ships scouting around the city barrier, with several more searching along the dock lanes.

"What the hell?!" They exclaimed in unison.

"Incoming ship!" A voice commanded over the speakers. "Please identify!"

Ash and Trixie looked at eachother worriedly before Ash grabbed the microphone.

"This is Amelia Traechart in the Pixie 6-9. Just going for a cruise."

Trixie looked up her in a mix of confusion and impression.

"Well the spaceport is under lockdown at the moment." The voice replied.

"Can I ask why?" Ashlynn asked.

"You may." The voice responded casually. "There was an attack in the city, 212 citizens dead! For saftey and security all docks are closed."

"T-thank you for the warning o-officer." Ashlynn choked.

"Stay safe out there, traveller!" The voice added.

Without another word Ash dropped the microphone and slammed her fist into the wall, tears rolling down her cheeks.

Trixie remained silent as her friend slowly collapsed in tears. After several moments Ashlynn snapped upwards and grabbed the controls. She banked the ship back around torward an open dock and put it at full speed.

Trixie screamed.

"ASH WHAT ARE YOU DOING?!"

After shooting past the security checkpoint, Ashlynn slammed the ship down through the atrium ceiling and dropped into the transit tunnels at the bottom of the atrium.

"ASH WHAT THE FUCK?!" Trixie yelled.

"DOCKS ARE CLOSED REMEMBER!" Ash mocked, running through the hatch.

Trixie followed her as they raced up the empty tunnel and down the maintenence corridor. As they came across a server room, Ash kicked the door in.

"Ash what the..." Trixie began.

"Keep them busy, Trix!" Ash interrupted.

Without a grumbled sigh metallic tendrils slid from her underbody as she spun around. Her tail stiffening as it's claw blossomed open, revealing a lens, watching the opposite direction.

While Trixie kept watch, Ash furiously typed away at the holographic screen, causing more and more to appear as she searched through the security database.

"Anything?" Trixie asked.

"Nothing yet." Ash huffed. "How are we looking out there?"

"No targets." Trixie sighed annoyed.

After a moment she tensed up as Ashlynn exclaimed worriedly behind her.

"Holy shit!"

"What?" Trixie asked. "What happened?"

"Look." Ash replied in tears.

The largest screen was playing a news clip.

A female reporter spoke as the background displayed various warnings.

"Not long ago there was an attack on building six-one in the plaza district. Witnesses claim the missle was fired from a limousine, which then fired another missle into the water near the riverfront district and fled the area."

A smaller screen appeared in the feed, showing Jace's limo outrunning both of the explosions.

The reporter continued.

"Authorities claim they cut power to the grid controller beforehand, causing a city wide traffic jam."

Ash paused the feed, collapsing to the floor in tears.

"He was in that building, I know he was!"

"Ash." Trixie sighed. "I'm so sorry."

Comforting her, Trixie glared at the screen. Her eyes bouncing around until something caught her attention.

"Wait a minute." She whispered.

After studying it for a second, she quickly reassured Ash.

"Ash he's not dead." she exclaimed.

"Bullshit!" Ash cried.

"Look!" Trixie said, pointing a tendril.

Studying the paused image, Ash saw nothing.

"Trixie what the..."

"Right there!" Trixie interupted.

Looking closer, Ash could see Jace in the back of the limo, crying.

"He's alive?" She asked happily, as her voice turned to anger. "He was attacked?!"

Picking herself up, Ash rewound the feed and let it play.

"Pause it!" Trixie exclaimed, pointing again.

"Zoom in on that missle." She added.

After zooming in, they both gasped as the insignia on the missle became clear.

"You've got to be shitting me!" They exclaimed in unison.

They cautiously played the feed.

After the explosion, the screen dissappeared and the reporter continued.

"Their whereabouts are curently unknown, however witnesses claim they escaped through the city's atmospheric barrier..."

"THERE!" A guard shouted.

Without a word, Ash grabbed her pistol and fired a shot as a guard came to the door. The guard flew backwards as the bolt impacted his chest.

"We gotta go!" Ash said, grabbing her things.

"What about the..." Trixie asked.

"NOW!" Ash screamed, hopping on her saddle.

As they took off back towards the ship, security drones came marching around the corner.

"BASTARDS!" Ashlynn yelled.

Trixie drifted around and took off the other way as the drones opened fire.

"How are we gonna find him now!" She asked.

"I'm thinking." Ash replied.

As they rode through the maintenance corridors gaurds began coming around the corners.

"THINK FAST!" Trixie shouted.

Ash thought for a second.

"Take that next hall back to the transit tunnel!"

Halfway to the corner, a platoon of guards came pouring out, weapons ablaze.

"SHIT!" They yelled.

In a split second, Trixie launched herself over the volley of plasma. By the time the guards redirected their fire, Trixie had bounced of the wall and dissappeared up the adjacent hallway.

As another platoon formed ahead, She launched herself torwards the wall and released her tyre spikes, sticking them to the wall while Ash put her handlebars in a death grip.
She screamed excitedly as they sped along..
"STOP SCREWING AROUND!" Ash demanded.
Trixie leapt off the wall, landing behind the platoon, and rounded the next corner. Nearing a corridor intersection, they noticed another squad forming ahead.
"KILL THEM?" Trixie asked.
"SLAP 'EM!" Ash shouted.
Trixie slid 180 degrees, whipping her tail through the group of drones, slcing them in half. As they raced ahead to the ship, Ash's communicator beeped.
"I FOUND HIM!" She gasped happily.
"WHERE?!" Trixie replied.
"I'll tell you on the way!" Ash chuckled happily.
Before the hatch was fully closed, the ship had already bust another hole in the atrium roof and rocketed away from the spaceport, barely avoiding the security shuttles.

Chapter 7

Jace and Miranda stood across from the podium, as the Captain examined the files. Two guards stood watch over the empty room. Miranda fidgeted nervously, as the Captain glanced at her every few seconds.

"Do you mind explaining this?" He demanded.

"We were attacked, Captain." Miranda replied.

"I am aware of that, Officer Briggswelle." The captain said plainly.

Jacen and Miranda stood silent as The captain pulled up a holographic screen.

The footage showed their limo flying through the city evading a missles.

After pausing the footage, The captain spoke.

"That first missle took out 212 people. Why?"

Miranda swallowed hard as the Captain glared at her.

"Answer me Briggeswelle!" The Captain commanded.

"I..." Miranda shivered in fear. "I was just trying to get my target to saftey, Captain."

The Captain rubbed his nose in frustration.

"Then would you mind explaining why you were alone with the target?" He asked.

Miranda shook nervously.

"Briggswelle!" The Captain demanded.

"S-saftey, Captain." She replied.

"Safety?" He asked.

She cleared her throat.

"Yes, Captain Mordis." Miranda continued. "I wanted to be sure he..."

"THAT IS A SHITTY EXCUSE!" The Captain interupted.
She went quiet.
"THIS WAS SUPPOSED TO BE A STEALTH OPERATION, BRIGGSWELLE!" Captain Mordis shouted angrily. "212 PEOPLE ARE DEAD AND HALF THE CITY IS IN LOCKDOWN!"
Miranda struggled to remain composed as she choked back tears.
"I want you in my office after you get done interogating this piece of shit!" Captain Mordis Growled.
Jacen took a breath.
"Captain, Sir..."
Captain Mordis pulled a gun and fired a shot into the ceiling before walking over to Jace and putting the warm barrel in his mouth.
"You'll be lucky if you get jail time after this is all over! GOT IT!?"
Jacen nodded fearfully.
Captain Mordis then looked over to Miranda.
"Briggswelle!"
"Y-Yes, Captain?" She squeaked.
"Get every last piece of information you can out of this shit-bag then get straight to my office!"
"Y-yes, Captain." She squeaked again.
"LOUDER!" He shouted.
"YES CAPTAIN!" Miranda yelled back.
"Good!" He replied.
He walked over and grabbed the files, then handed them to Miranda before turning to leave. As he walked away Miranda saluted, followed by Jacen.
Captain Mordis stood for a moment before stepping over to Jace again.
"Have you served, Mr. Ahd?" He asked.
"No sir." Jace replied.
"Did you enlist?" The Captain continued.
"No sir." Jace replied again.

"THEN YOU ARE A CIVILIAN!" The Captain shouted. "AND I WILL NOT TOLERATE YOUR DISRESPECT! NOW LOWER YOUR HAND!"

Jace quickly pulled his hand to his side, and stood fast.

"Sorry sir!" He said, shaking.

"CALL ME SIR ONE MORE TIME AND I WILL HAVE BOTH YOUR ASSES THROWN OUT THE AIRLOCK! IS THAT CLEAR?"

"YES CAPTAIN!" They shouted in unison.

"NOW GET THIS MESS CLEANED UP!" He yelled.

The Captain walked off, as he and the guards left the room, Jace took a sigh of relief.

"Miranda look..."

Miranda struck him in the face.

"JACKASS!" She yelled.

He winced.

"What the hell was..."

She struck him again, knocking him to the floor.

"Are you trying to get us killed?" She shouted.

"What the hell?" Jace exclaimed.

"That is Captain Salazar Mordis!" She fumed.

"Who?" He asked.

She cocked her fist again.

"Wait, hold on!" He said, raising his hands. "I didn't know."

She sighed heavy, tears rolled down her cheeks.

"I-I don't want to hear another word until we get to my office, dipshit!

After picking himself up off the floor, Miranda led him out of the room in silence. After a while they came across what looked like a janitors closet. As Miranda unlocked it she motioned Jacen into a small room. On one side was a well made bed next to a nightstand, decorated with various trinkets. On the other side was a small desk, with a hand carved plaque reading; "C.O.I: M.R. Briggswelle".

"Nice." Jace commented.

"Shut up and sit down." She replied coldly.

They quietly took their seats.

"Jacen, look." Miranda said. We're in deep shit here. I can't make you any promises, so just tell me what you know and I'll see what I can do.

"I'm gonna die, aren't I?" He asked fearfully, tears rolling down his cheek.

She pulled a file out of the folder and handed it to Jace with a heavy sigh.

"Here."

Jace hesitantly grabbed it.

As he studied it, his heart sunk, blood falling from his cheeks.

"Recognise it?" She asked.

The file contained a fully detailed scematic, of his design.

"Y-yeah." Jace replied, glancing up.

"You understand now, right?" She asked softly.

"This doesn't make any sense." He said.

She quietly slid the entire folder over.

Without a word, he began looking through it, placing each file on the desk. His breath deepening with each one. As he pulled out the last file, tears began rolling down his cheek. Jace held up his scematic and placed it in the center.

On the desk before him were several weapon blueprints, each one detailing it's damage and targets.

Cupping his mouth, Jace cowered out of the chair, choking back tears.

"I didn't know, I-I swear."

Miranda stood to her feet.

"Jacen..."

"You gotta believe me." He cried harder. "Please."

As he curled up on the floor, Miranda hesitated to comfort him.

"Damnit." She sighed.

He shuttered as Miranda placed a hand on his shoulder.

"I believe you Jace, I do." She cooed. "Now please get up."
"Really?" He squeaked.
"Yes..., really." She replied softly.
After a moment he caught his breath, as Miranda helped him up. She then gave him a box of tissues.
"You're gonna be okay." She said. "I promise."
"Can I have a moment alone, please?" He whimpered.
After a brief silence, She placed a hand on his shoulder.
"10 minutes." She sighed. "Okay?"
"Thank you." Jace replied softly.
As she closed the door, Jace broke down crying again. Thoughts running through his mind at a breakneck pace. He cupped his face and sobbed even harder. After several minutes, he wiped away tears and sat by the porthole.
The galaxies and distant stars glimmered like a dream, a new life, gone before it even started. His heart sunk deep as he dropped his head. He then saw the wristband. The lines were shifting in a soft, rythmic pattern, like they were trying to calm him. Then he saw more words forming. He watched in silent awe as the bracelet spoke with him.
"NEED HELP?"
He giggled in a mix of shock and joy.
"Ash you clever bitch." He spoke quietly. "Time for some fun."
With a sigh of hope and desperation, he pressed the emergency button firmly.

Chapter 8

Ash woke up to soft beeping. With a powerful yawn she grabbed the communicator and examined it.

"TRIXE!" She yelled.

"Ash I'm right here." She replied. "What's up?"

"We just got another S.O.S!" Ash exclaimed.

"Where?!" Trixie asked happily.

Ash stepped out of her chair, holding the device as she turned around the cabin.

"6 lightyears, due.. that way!" She pointed. "Moving?"

"Those sons of bitches ain't geting away that easily!" Trixie cursed, veering the ship.

"When I get my hands on..." Ash paused.

"DAMNIT!" She growled.

She slammed her head against the wall in anger.

"ASH,WHAT?" Trixie shouted.

Ash quietly laughed in shock as tears began pouring down her cheeks.

"What is it?" Trixie asked worriedly.

"I could've called him." Ash giggled sadly.

Trixie began chortling softly.

"IT'S NOT FUNNY!" Ash shouted. "I THOUGHT HE WAS DEAD!"

Trixie laughed harder as she slid out of her chair.

"SHUT THE HELL UP TRACER!" Ash shouted.

With a hook, She punched the cyborg in the head several times.

"I WAS SCARED!" Ash growled. "I COULDN'T THINK RIGHT!"

Trixie's laughter quickly turned to crying as she collapsed to the floor.

"Trixie?" Ash worried.

She was crying too hard to answer. Ash knelt down, placing a hand on her saddle.

"Trix, I'm sorry." She apologised. "I didn't mean to..."

"I'LL KILL 'EM!" Trixie screamed. "THEY'RE AS GOOD AS DEAD!"

Ash rubbed her friends saddle assuringly.

"I just miss him, Ash!" Trixie cried. "I miss him so much."

Ash grabbed the communicator and softly teased her.

"I missed him too, Trix."

"Feeling better?" Miranda asked.

"Kinda." Jace replied.

"This whole thing is a shit show." She said worriedly. "But I'll do what I can so you don't get killed."

"Thanks." He sighed hopelessly.

Miranda shuffled the papers back into the folder.

"So you had no idea?" She asked.

"Not really." Jace muttered.

Miranda sighed in agreement as she pulled up a holographic screen.

"Let's just get this out of the way."

"Sure." Jace muttered again.

"You're were contacted by this company, yes?" She asked.

"Yes." He replied.

"They were looking for an engineer and offered you a job. Yes?"

He nodded.

"You submitted a design for the power amplifier, yes?"

He nodded again.

"You were told it was for starships, not weaponry, yes?"

He nodded once more.

"You had no further involvment, yes?"
"Yes. He sighed again.
"Okay." Miranda said. "That's done."
As she minimized the screen, Jace relaxed in his chair.
"So what were those attacks about?" He asked casually.
Miranda huffed softly.
"I honestly couldn't tell you Jacen."
"Whatever." Jacen quipped softly.
"Look here, Mr. Jacen Thaddeus Ahd!" Miranda growled. "My life was
in danger too! The last thing I wanted to do was get people killed!"
Tears rolled down Jace's cheek as he slumped over.
"I never should have left."
"Well you,re here now, Jacen." Miranda replied coldly. "We both are."
They looked at eachother in silent agreement.
"That does leave me wondering though." She continued.
"The attacks?" Jacen asked.
"Yeah." She replied curiously. "It was either a set up, or a tip off."
They sat wondering.
"Only two people know I went undercover." She continued. "My inside
girl, and Captain Mordis."
Just then, The bracelet started glowing as a button appeared.
Miranda leaned over the desk for a better look.
"What the hell is that?" She asked curiously.
"Backup!" Jace replied.
As he hit the button and spoke, she worried silently.
"Backup?"

Chapter 9

"Ash? Trixie?" Jace answered.
"JACEN!" They exclaimed in unison.
"Are you alright?" Ash worried.
"Did they hurt you?" Trixie added.
Jace let off a sigh of relief.
"Boy am I glad to hear from you two!"
"Jace!" Trixie asked worriedly. "Did anyone hurt you?"
He thought for a second.
"Well no, but..."
"THEY BETTER NOT HAVE!" Trixie threatened.
"Is anyone there now?" Ash demanded.
"Yeah." Jace replied. "I..."
"IF YOU MOTHERFUCKERS TOUCH HIM YOU'RE DEAD!"
Trixie shouted.
"I'LL USE YOUR SKULLS..."
"TRIXE! ASH!" Jace interupted. "I'M FINE!"
There was a brief silence.
"You swear?" Ash huffed.
"Absolutley." He replied.
Miranda motioned to get his attention.
"Jace, where are you?" Ash asked.
"I..." He replied. "I'm on a ship."
Miranda motioned harder.
"Which one?" Trixie asked.
"I'm on the..., hold on." He paused.
Jace held the his wristband away from his face.

"Miranda." He asked softly. "What's this ship?"

"Jace we can't give away our location." She replied. "Are you fucking crazy?"

"We can trust them." He said.

"This is fucking serious right now." She quietly exclaimed. "Mordis is going to kill us if he finds out!"

"They can help." He said.

"We're already in deep shit as it is." She answered. "Are you trying to get us killed?! We don't don't need any goddamn help!"

She grabbed the communicator from him.

"It's fine." He exclaimed. "Once they get..."

Jace paused, his face turning white.

"Holy shit!" Miranda exclaimed. "Are you okay?"

He motioned for the wristband. As she handed it over, He snapped it from her.

"A-Ash, were are you?" He stuttered.

"JACE!?" Trixie screamed.

Alarms started blaring all over the ship!

"I'm on the..., hold on." Jace paused.

Ash and Trixie nervously pulled the device closer. They could hear Jace talking with someone, but couldn't make it out.

"I don't like this Trixie." Ash said.

"Me neither." She replied. "Jace?"

"Jace!" Ash commanded.

They could still hear him talking.

"You think he heard us?" Trixie asked.

"There!" Ash exclaimed.

She pointed out the viewscreen, to a massive ship in the distance.

"Is that a G.P.S warship?" Trixie worried.

"Jace get to an escape pod," Ash commanded. "We're opening fire!"

Trixie gasped in shock.
"ASH! What are you..., we don't even have any weapons on this thing!"
"We have a targeting system, don't we?" Ash teased.
"It's fine." Jace exclaimed.
"Jace!" Trixie gasped. "How..."
"Holy shit, Are you okay?" A young woman shouted.
Trixie grabbed the communicator, listening close, as targeting reticules appeared on the viewscreen.
"A-Ash, where are you?" Jace asked worriedly.
"JACE!?" Trixie screamed.
"LOCKED!" Ash growled.

Chapter 10

"ASH!" Jace repeated.

"Jace are you okay?" Trixie answered.

"What is she doing Trixie!?" He asked frantically.

"Targeting the ship!" She replied.

Miranda grabbed the wristband, shouting into it frantically.

"ARE YOU TRYING TO START A WAR!?"

"WHEN I'M DONE," Ash screamed back. "THERE WON'T BE ENOUGH OF YOU LEFT FOR A WAR!"

"Trixie please tell me she's bluffing!" Jace cried.

"Jace, you need to find an escape pod." Trixie commanded. "NOW!"

Miranda threw the wristband back at Jace, and shouted mockingly.

"CAN WE TRUST THEM TO OPEN FIRE?!"

"We gotta go!" Jace said.

He grabbed his bag, as Miranda grabbed the other strap.

"We?!" She scoffed.

"You saved my ass!" Jace replied. "Now let me save yours!"

He reached for her hand, but she flipped it and grabbed his instead.

"She justs want you, right?" She asked.

"She's still gonna fire." Jace replied.

Miranda loosened her grip, still clutching his wrist.

"I was doing my job!" She exclaimed.

Captain Mordis began shouting over the loudspeakers.

"BRIGGSWELLE! I KNOW YOU HAD SOMETHING TO DO WITH THIS! GET YOUR ASS TO THE BRIDGE NOW, GODDAMNIT!"

"And I'm doing you a favor!" Jace replied..

She hesitated, before releasing her grip.

"FUCK IT!" She screamed.

She collected the files, smashing them into a rucksack.

"Is that it?" Jace asked.

"Yes!" She replied. " Now let's move!"

"SOMEONE GET ME BRIGGSWELLE NOW!" Captain Mordis yelled.

As they sprinted down the hall, the sound of blaster fire rang out behind them, as plasma bolts flew past.

"BASTARD!" Miranda screamed. "Jace, how long?"

"5 minutes, tops!" He replied. "Why?"

"Follow me!" She asnwered.

She grabbed his hand and pulled him down a side hall.

"Jump!" She yelled.

"Are you crazy?" Jace yelled. "It's a dead end!"

"It's a drop-shaft." She replied. "It's leads straight to the hangar!"

The wall and floor split open, revealing a hidden shaft. Miranda gripped his hand tighter and leapt into it, with him in tow. A few seconds later, their fall was broken by a rush of air, that carried them into the hangar bay.

As their feet touched the floor, they took off sprinting past a row of cargo shuttles.

"These aren't escape pods!" Jace exclaimed.

"They're better!" Miranda replied.

They came to a stop near the largest shuttle. Seconds after she pulled up a keypad, the door slid open.

In the blink of an eye, she grabbed Jace and tossed him inside.

As the door closed, Miranda jumped into the center chair and grabbed the control yoke. As the shuttle began lifting off the floor, plasma bolts impacted the shields.

As waves of energy danced along the viewscreen, Miranda rotated the shuttle towards the hangar door. Several targeting reticules appeared, and began locking on to it. Jace was stricken with fear.

"MIRANDA WHAT ARE YOU..."

"KNOCK KNOCK, MOTHERFUCKER!" She cackled.

Two pairs of missles flew into the door!

As it exploded out into space, shuttles and personnel began flying out. After manuevering their shuttle past the debri and out of the hangar, Miranda spun it around, bringing the warship on screen, as more reticules appeared.

"MIRANDA ARE YOU FUCKING CRAZY?!" Jace screamed.

"WHAT THE HELL ARE YOU DOING?!"

"GETTING REVENGE!" She screamed.

Chapter 11

"JACE!" Trixie screamed. "SOMEONE'S ATTACKING THE SHIP, GET OUT OF THERE NOW!"

"TRIXIE THAT'S US!" Ash and Jace replied in unison.

"WHAT?!" She screamed.

"WHERE AM I DOCKING?" Miranda yelled.

"Jace who was that?" Ash demanded

"Briggswelle!" Miranda replied. "Now where the hell am I docking?"

"Uhm, Jace?" Trixie quivered.

"Look, She's flying this thing." He answered. "Where the hell are you guys?"

There was a brief moment of silence.

"There!" Miranda exclaimed.

She pointed to a shuttle in the distance.

"Are you guys in that shuttle?" He asked.

"Y-yeah!" Ash replied. "We'll lead you to the ship!"

"You're gonna love it!" Trixie added.

The communication cut off, as Ash grabbed the communicator from Trixie.

"SHIT!" They screamed.

"IS HE FUCKING CRAZY?" Ash yelled.

"TOLD YOU THIS WAS A BAD IDEA!" Trixie shouted.

"YOU DIDN'T SAY ANYTHING!" Ash screamed.

"I didn't need to say anything for you to realize IT'S A BAD IDEA TO THREATEN A GALACTIC PATROL WARSHIP!" Trixie exclaimed. "WITHOUT ANY FUCKING WEAPONS!"

She slammed a tire down in anger.

"WHAT WAS I SUPPOSED TO DO TRIXIE?" Ash replied.
"NOT THREATEN THEM?!" She said sarcastically.
"FUCK YOU!" Ash retorted.
"Now we have the attention of the FREAKING GLALACTIC PATROL!" Trixie shouted. "And one psycho bitch!"
"Trixie, this is bad." Ash said. "This is really freaking bad!"
"Agreed." Trixie replied.
"Let's just get Jace out of there first." Ash sighed.
After catching their breath, they sat back down, as a massive luxury shuttle began dropping in front of them.
"Oh shit!" They exclaimed.
As the viewscreen leveled out with their own, they could see a petite, uniformed girl sitting at the control yoke. Jace was strapped into the seat next to her.
He held up the wirstband, pressing the call button as he gave a thumbs up.
"You guys went silent and stopped." He began. "We need to go, Now!"
"J-just follow us." Ash replied.
Miranda grabbed the wristband from Jace.
"You guys seem alright." She commented. "I owe you a drink."
"Anytime." Ash cleared her throat.
"Look, I really don't want to sound like a bitch now." Miranda continued. "But we need to get the hell out of here!"
"Yeah...Yes. Yes of course!" Ash replied. "We calling our ship now."
"Lead the way!" Miranda said.
As she handed the wristband to Jace, The patchwork ship rotated and sped onward. Miranda followed close.
"Ash what the hell?" Trixie whispered.
Ash grabbed the communicator and cut the line.
"Trixie this just went from bad to worse." She whimpered.
"Ash I know." She replied. "Now what do we do?"

Ash pondered for a moment, looking around the cabin, then back to the view screen.

"I'm thinking of a plan." She said. "We just need to keep them distracted for now."

"ARE YOU FUCKING CRAZY?" Trixie shouted. "THAT THING HAS WEAPONS, AND WHO KNOWS WHAT ELSE!"

"I'M WORKING ON IT TRIXIE!" Ash yelled back. "NOW GET OFF MY ASS!"

The communicator beeped again.

"Look, just keep them distracted for now." She pleaded. "Okay?"

Trixie answered the call, as she whispered to Ash.

"Crazy bitch!"

Chapter 12

"So she tossed me in," Jace explained. "and blew the freaking hangar door off!"

"In his personal shuttle?" Trixie asked, faking amazement.

"I like to travel in style." Miranda bragged. "Plus, it has a mini-bar."

"Save me some!" Ash replied.

They all chuckled for a moment.

"Hey Jace?" Ash said. "We'll call you right back."

The line went dead, as She nearly crushed the device.

"We fucked up!" Ash exclaimed. "This is getting out of control."

"And why is that?" Trixie replied sarcastically.

Ash grumbled as she clenched her fist, staring daggers at Trixie. After a few deep breaths, she relaxed.

"Because now we have an intelligence officer following us in a stolen shuttle, which was used to attack a G.P.S warship, Jace is sitting next to her, and we still need to find our own goddamn ship!"

"So what do we do now?" Trixie asked.

"Find a goddamn ship!" Ash rebuttled.

They went silent. The only sound being the hum of the engines and a few beeps from the readout cluster.

"What about the Pegasus?" Trixie suggested.

"Perfect!" Ash gasped.

"I'm on it." Trixie replied.

She grabbed another device and began flicking through holograms, After several minutes, She lowered it with a worried sigh.

"Okay, I have bad news, and worse news."

"What's the worst?" Ash demanded.

The communicator beeped as plasma flew past the shuttles.

"THAT!" Trixie screamed.

She snapped the communicator from Ash.

"You drive, I'll talk!" She paused. "Jace, what's...

"HOW FAR IS YOUR DAMN SHIP?" Miranda shouted!

"Just ahead, hang on!" Trixie reassured.

"My captain found us, and He's coming fast." Miranda continued. "WE NEED TO GO NOW!"

"ASH," Jace yelled. "PLEASE TELL ME YOU GUYS HAVE A PLAN!"

She thought for a moment. Looking over the readouts, as Trixie read the device.

"Okay, Trix." She huffed. "What's the bad news?"

"Start heading to Tenamora!" Trixie replied.

"Tenamora?!" Ash exclaimed. "Trixie that's..."

"The ship is there," She commanded. "NOW GO!"

"ASH!" Jace and Miranda cried in unison.

"HYPERDRIVE!" Trixie screamed.

"WHAT?" They replied.

"Does that thing have hyper drive?" She shouted.

"Yeah, Why?" Miranda asked.

"Input these coordinates," Trixie commanded. "We're jumping now!"

Jace typed the coordinates into the shuttle's computer as fast as Trixie said them, with the plasma fire increasing heavily.

"Okay Trixie, they're in!" He exclaimed.

"THE SHIP IS THERE!" She yelled. "NOW JUMP!"

Their ship raced ahead as light began warping and bending around the hull, seconds later they disappeared in a blinding flash, sending ripples of energy outward.

"DOES SHE ALWAYS DO SHIT LIKE THIS?!" Miranda exclaimed.

"I REALLY FUCKING HOPE SO!" Jace yelled. "NOW COME ON!"

Seconds later, they followed suite and disappeared into the ripples.

Chapter 13

The patchwork ship appeared in a flash of light, far above a desert planet. They drifted for a moment, looking for the others.

"There!" Trixie pointed.

Energy ripples expanded and pulsed faster before the shuttle came rocketing past.

As they shot towards the planet, Ash and Trixie followed close behind.

"Not bad you guys!" Ash commented.

"THIS IS FUCKING TERRIBLE!" Miranda shouted.

"Why?" Trixie asked.

The shuttle burst into flame as it hit the atmosphere, sending bits and pieces flying off.

"BECAUSE WE JUST LOST CONTROL!" Miranda screamed.

Jace could be heard cursing in the background as Miranda continued.

"THAT STUPID JUMP OF YOURS FRIED OUR CONTROL SYSTEMS AND DRAINED OUR FUEL!"

"HOW?" Ash screamed.

"LIKE HELL IF I KNOW!" Miranda quipped. "NOW GET OVER HERE AND SAVE US!"

Ash spun the shuttle around and took off after the derelict vessel. As they neared the craft, the flames danced and flickered along the hull, threatening to jump from one craft to the other.

"Trixie I have an idea!" Ash commanded.

She grumbled in annoyance.

"Don't tell me, please."

The ship's hatch hissed open as Trixie climbed out. Digging her claws and tires into the hull, she climbed to the bottom. As they became level with the shuttle She lowered herself onto their hull, digging her tires in.

"I'M CONNECTED!" Trixie screamed.

Soft crunching could be heard inside the shuttle, as Miranda and Jace struggled to hang on.

"What the hell was that?" Miranda shouted.

The wirstband vibrated and beeped as Jace answered.

"Everybody hang tight!" Ash yelled.

Outside the viewscreen, they could see the nose of Ash's ship a few feet ahead. Fire danced around the vessels as they entered the planet's atmosphere. Diving towards the ground, Ash fought to keep the ships level, pulling Trixie taut. As they dropped below the clouds, a massive cave entrance came into view, in the center of a moutain range.

As the wind and turbulence died down, Trixie could be heard screaming and cursing wildly as the cave entrance grew in size.

Bringing the shuttles to a hover just inside, Ash began to descend as Trixie released her grip on the upper craft, dropping Miranda, Jace and herself to cave floor below.

As they bounced around inside, Trixie rolled down the nose of the shuttle in a red hot ball, coming to a stop in a stop just in front. Without hesitation, Jace opened the hatch and went running over to her, Miranda followed him with her pistols drawn.

Trixie was covered in glowing red panels, panting heavily. Her suspension and tendrils were stretched into a loose pile.

As the the other shuttle landed nearby, Miranda bolted over to the hatch, as it opened with a cloud of steam.

"FREEZE!" She commanded.

Ash stopped in her tracks, hands held high.

"Hey, whoa." She hesitated. "No need to..."

"Shut it!" Miranda interupted. "Remove all your weapons now!"

A few metallic thumps could be heard as Ash dropped her weapons to the shuttle floor. She slowly walked out, hands still raised.

Miranda stepped over to greet her.
"After all that," She continued. "That's still, one hell of an introduction!"
Ash swallowed as she moved closer. Weapons still drawn.
"You, must be Ash."

Chapter 14

Tension grew in the air as they stared eachother down.

"There was no ship," Miranda started. "Was there?"

"Okay, look." Ash stuttered. "It's in this..."

"Or weapons?" Miranda continued.

Ash stood silent, as Miranda held the pistols inches from her face.

"Miranda?" Jace called worriedly.

She took a deep breath.

"You threatened a glactic patrol warship with the targeting system of an outdated shuttle?"

Ash swallowed hard as the barrels lined up with her eyes.

"Y-yes." She choked. "H-how did you..."

"Shut it!" Miranda commanded.

There was a moment of silence as She relaxed herself.

"Impressive." She continued. "Crazy and stupid, I like that."

"Uh..., Thanks." Ash replied.

She slowly tensed up in anger, as Miranda closely eyed her, lowering her weapons.

"Have we, met before?" Miranda asked.

"I hope so." Ash joked quietly.

There was an eeire moment of silence, as they looked eachother in the eye.

"So where is this ship of yours?" Miranda asked.

Trixie grunted and winced, as she pulled herself back together.

"I need to make sure she's okay!" Ash replied.

As she ran over to Trixie, Miranda strolled along behind her.

"You two alright?" Ash asked, faking it.

"Ash you better have a damn good plan!" Trixie grunted.

As she rolled over onto her tires, she took several deep breaths as her tendrils brushed off dirt. The panels quickly returned to normal as they cooled.

"So now what?" Jace asked.

"Now." Ash started. "We need to..."

"WHOA!" Miranda exclaimed.

Everyone nervously spun around as She paced over to Trixie.

Miranda excitedly checked her out, as she watched in a mix of irritation and anger.

She slowly reached for a claw.

"What are these?"

"My hands." Trixie grumbled, pulling it away.

"So, what are you?" Miranda asked curiously. "Some kind of..."

"JACE!" Trixie gasped.

She whipped around, pulling her tail away from his light grip.

"Sore!" She exclaimed. "I am very sore!"

She quickly rolled over behind Ash.

"Can we just find the damn ship, Please?!"

Ash looked down at her, then back to Jace and Miranda.

"You guys should stay here." She began. "Our crew doesn't like outsiders."

"What?" Miranda asked.

"Look." Trixie added. "We'll find the ship, you guys just relax."

Jace looked at her for a second.

"Ash, I thought you..."

"For saftey." She interrupted.

"Just stay here, please." Trixie groaned.

"Alright." Miranda sighed. "Just make it quick."

Without a word, Ash hopped on Trixie's back as she winced and grunted. Beams of light shot from her eyes as the whine of her motors faded into the distance.

As they raced deeper into the cave, Ash huffed angrily.
"Goddamnit!"
"This is bullshit." Trixie added
"You think she knows?" Ash asked.
"Can we just find the ship first?" Trixie replied.
They remained silent as the darkness intensified.
"We have to kill her." Ash sighed. "This is getting dangerous."
"You say that like we haven't done this before." Trixie quipped. "But yes, That bitch is somehting else."

"Are they always like that?" Miranda asked. "They seem tense."
"Miranda, your guess is as good as mine." Jace replied.

Chapter 15

After some time, The pair came across a massive ship, nestled in an alcove near the back of the cave. Strips of soft neon light ran along it's length, faintly iluminating the outer hull.
"Hell of a parking job." Trixie quipped. "How do you think they did it?"
"We'll ask inside," Ash grumbled. "now shut up!"
A holographic keypad materialized in front of Ash, as she stepped over to the entrance hatch. After she typed in a code, the pad flashed from Blue to Red and back.
"The hell?" She quipped. "My code isn't working."
"Try mine." Trixie said.
The screen flashed once more.
"Damn." Ash cursed softly.
"Whittle's?" Trixie suggested.
The screen flashed red again.
Ash cursed in frustration.
"Son of a..."
"BITCH!" A voice shouted.
"WHITTLE!?" They both answered.
In the blink of an eye, a large figure came flying out of the darkness and tackled Ash to the ground. Tumbling through the dust, they came to a stop under a light strip. Driving fist after fist into Ash, Whittle cried in anger.
"5 YEARS!"
"Whittle!" Trixie exclaimed.

As she rolled closer, Whittle redirected a fist into Trixie's side, sending her into the darkness.
"5 GODDAMN YEARS, ASH!" Whittle screamed.
"Whittle." She choked.
"WE THOUGHT YOU WERE DEAD!" She cried.

Jace and Miranda explored around the shuttles as they waited.
"Does this, feel weird," Miranda asked. "Or is it just me?"
"What?" Jace asked.
"This whole situation." Miranda continued. "It just feels..., off."
"Yeah." Jace replied. "Ash has that effect."
"Well, whatever then." Miranda said. "Come on."
She stepped into their shuttle, and took seat at the table. Jace sat across from her, as she looked over the files.
After a moment, she grabbed her rucksack, and began rummaging through it. Seconds later, she jumped up from the table with a horrified gasp.
"FUCK!"
"What?" Jace asked worriedly.
"That SON OF A BITCH!" Miranda shouted.
She ran over to the sink, and started ripping the panels off. Then she cocked her fist and drove it into the wall.
After a moment of rummaging through the internals, she ripped out a palm sized device and crushed it.
"This is bad!" She exclaimed. "That was a tracker!"
"Miranda, it just got worse." Jace added.
She perked up, and looked over. But before she saw anyting, He tackled her into the rear bedroom.
"LOOK OUT!"
As they landed on the bed, Jace cupped her mouth, and leaned into her ear.

"There is something very big out there. And it know's we're in here."
In the silence, They could hear the faint crunch of rock and gravel just
outside. Miranda slowly moved his hand away from her lips.
"There are twin cannons in the closet." She whispered back.
"What?" Jace quietly exclaimed.
Miranda quickly cupped his mouth.
"Shut it you moron." She continued. "That's all we got for defense."
A loud grunt could be heard, as the crunching stopped.
"Move, NOW!" She commanded.
She pressed him and herself against the back wall.
Moments later, they were tossed about the room, as an ear shattering
crunch destroyed the roof. They quickly got to their feet, and grabbed
the weapons.
"FIRE ON MY COMMAND!" She yelled.

Whittle cried softly into Ash's breasts.
"Whittle, we're sorry." Ash sighed. "But it wasn't our fault."
Whittle only cried harder, softly pounding her chest.
"It's not fair!" She wept. "It's just not FAIR!"
"Whittle, Listen." Trixie commanded. " We'll explain later, but we
need help. Where's...?"
A deafening roar of pain echoed throughout the cave, followed the
sound of heavy blaster fire.
"RX!" They cried in unison.

Chapter 16

With all her strength, Miranda sent the creature flying backwards with a kick.

"NOT SO TOUGH NOW, ARE YA?!" She taunted.

She got a running start and bodyslammed it.

"Miranda please stop!" Jace begged. "I think it's dead."

"IT'S NOT DEAD UNITL I SAY!" She screamed.

She got another running start and bodyslammed the creature again.

"RX!" Trixie and Whittle cried from the darkness.

"Jace!" Ash echoed behind them.

"Ash!" He shouted. "Hurry!"

Trixie's headlights blinded them as she sped closer.

Jace and Miranda could barely see Ash and the other figure riding Trixie. Leaping off, they both tumbled and rolled to their feet near the creature, as Trixie drifted to a halt near Miranda.

"RX, are you okay?" Whittle cried.

"What the hell is wrong with you?!" Ash demanded.

"She's just a kid!" Trixie added.

"What the hell are you talking about?" Miranda asked. "That thing just attacked us!"

"You shot her?!" Whittle cried.

"YOU WHAT?!" Ash and Trixie shouted in unison.

In the blink of an eye, Trixie tackled Miranda to ground and started lashing her tendrils. Ash piled on and started pummeling her.

Thinking fast, Jace grabbed a plasma rifle off the ground, Screaming frantically as he unloaded a full charge into the cave ceiling!

"WHAT THE HELL IS GOING ON!?" He cried angrily.

They paused. Trixie removed herself from the pile as Ash held Miranda down.

"Jace!" She began. "Look, we..."

"Trixie what the hell just happened?" He demanded.

Ash and Trixie glanced at eachother.

"She's a spy, Jace!" Ash began. "We..."

"Are lying!" Miranda shouted.

In the blink of an eye, She positioned her legs under Ash, and launched her over the patchwork Ship.

After picking herself up, She stepped over to Jace, as He pointed the gun at Trixie.

"I want some goddamn answers." He cried angrily. "NOW!"

As he looked over Miranda, he could faintly see bleeding lacerations all over her body. His hands started shaking as he kept the gun pointed at Trixie.

"Trixie!?" He tearfully demanded.

"Jace..." She choked. "She...".

"She what Trixie?" He demanded.

"She's a freaking G.P.S officer Jace." She cried.

"NOT ANYMORE!" Miranda shouted. "Thanks to your little stunt!"

"We thought he was in danger!" Trixie cried.

"On a patrol ship?" Miranda retorted.

"EVERYBODY SHUT UP!" Whittle cried. "She's trying to say something."

Everyone looked over at the crouched cyborg. The beast under her spasmed a little.

RX groaned, gently rubbing her side.

Miranda sighed apologetically.

"Look..., I'm..."

"Save it!" Whittle quipped, helping the beast up. "You idiots figure this out, I have to get her patched up."

They slowly paced deeper into the cave. As Ash came wobbling out of the darkness, Whittle sent her flying into the hull of the patchwork ship, with an anger filled strike.

"We thought he was kidnapped." Trixie sighed. "The attack was Ash's idea."

"I tried telling you guys I was safe." Jace said.

He lowered the weapon with a sigh.

"You know how she gets, Jace." Trixie rebuttled.

"You could have just pinged the ship." Miranda quipped.

"And tell them what? Officer Briggswelle." Trixie mocked.

"Oh, you know," Miranda shouted. "NOT THREATEN THEM FOR STARTERS!"

"WELL SORRY WE DIDN'T THINK OF THAT!" Trixie yelled.

"WELL YOUR STUPIDITY COST ME MY JOB!" Miranda shouted again. " AND I'M A GODDAMNED FUGITIVE NOW!"

"NO!" Trixie screamed. "IT WAS YOUR STUPIDITY THAT COST YOU YOUR JOB!"

Miranda huffed in anger.

"HIS DUMB ASS DRAGGED ME ALONG, BECAUSE HE THOUGHT YOU WERE DESTROYING THE SHIP!"

Trixie took a breath.

"WELL YOUR DUMBASS DID ENOUGH DAMAGE ALREADY! OFFICER: FIRE ON YOUR OWN DAMN SHIP!"

"ENOUGH!" Ash and Jace shouted in unison.

There was a moment of silence as they looked around, Ash pried herself off the hull and limped over.

"We were just trying to get him off the ship." She winced. "We didn't want you, and we didn't want trouble."

Miranda scoffed, and started crying angrily.

"You know, I hope you weren't kidding, Ash!"

Everyone remained silent as she continued.

"When you said there won't enough of them left for a war..."

Her crying shifted through a disturbing giggle, back to an angry tone.
"BECAUSE NOW WE'RE ALL IN TROUBLE!"
"What?" Trixe and Ash asked together.
"THERE WAS A TRACKER ON THE SHUTTLE!"
The air became palpable with tension, as fear and anger grew stronger.
"How did you idiots even find..." She paused.
She looked torwards Jace with a meancing scowl.
"Give me the wristband!" She demanded.
He struggled and hesitated to remove it, as she started walking over.
She held out an open hand as he pulled it off. After he placed it on her
palm, she crushed with a tiny shower of sparks, and opened her hand
again, revealing a mess of glowing circutry.
Before anyone could say anything, She punched Jace in the cheek as
hard as she could. A faint crack was heard, as he went flying into Ash,
who was sent back into the patchwork hull.
She then threw the wristband as hard as she could into the hull of the
other shuttle.
"WE'RE FUCKED!" She cried.
Trixie sighed in dispair.
"Miranda, we..."
"LEAVE ME ALONE! She screamed.
She paced out of the cave, into the baking heat.
After a moment, Trixie glanced around at the damage.
The wristband was embedded in the hull of one shuttle, Jace and Ash
were embedded in the hull of the other. The air reaked of sweat, hot
plasma and burnt fur.
Trixie sighed in defeat.
"This is gonna get so much worse, isn't it?"

Chapter 17

After placing a tube into Jace's cheek, Whittle gave him one last check.
"I don't know what the hell happened," She started. "But you two
better get this mess cleaned up."
Ash and Trixie glanced at eachother.
"Whittle, look." Ash began. "We..."
"Just...," She interrupted. "just don't, Ash."
Ash slumped onto Trixie's saddle. Tears started rolling her cheek.
"I was..."
"I don't care Ash." Whittle interrupted. "Not now anyway."
They went silent for a moment, as Whittle pondered quietly.
"Wasn't there a second idiot with you guys?"

Miranda shouted angrily into sky, as the alien sun baked her skin,
Throwing rocks and pebbles as hard as she could.
"I WAS JUST DOING MY DAMN JOB!" She cried, throwing
another stone.
"*Oh, you should join the Galactic Patrol.*" She cried to herself.
"That's a great idea, bro. We can be heros."
"*You should sign up for the super-soldier program.*"
"Even better, super-heros!"
"Then everyone will love us, AND WE WON'T END UP BAKING
TO DEATH ON A GODFORSAKEN DESERT PLANET!"
"DELTA YOU DRAINDEAD JACKASS!"
She threw another rock skyward.

"YOU NEVER EVEN ENLISTED YOU DIPSHIT!"
She clutched several more stones.
"BRING IT ON, MORDIS!"
She screamed, launching the pebbles skyward.
"YOU LIMPDICK MOTHERFUCKER!"
She collapsed to the ground in tears. Her skin red from sunburn, her muscles sore from throwing stones. She picked up a larger rock, the size of her head, and tearfully placed her forehead on it's hot surface.
"My life is just full of mistakes." She wept.

"She said there was a tracker!" Ash pondered.
As she stepped into the destroyed shuttle, bits and pieces of everything littered the floor.
"Here!" Ash exclaimed quietly.
She picked a small device off the floor. It looked like it had been crushed by a hydraulic press.
"What the hell?" She worried.
Looking around, she noticed several official papers scattered about.
Curious, she plucked one off a pile of fabric.
As she examined it, her breath quickened.
Jace's handwriting littered the page, around the image of a strange device.
One after another, she grabbed the papers, and scoured them intensely, until tears formed in her eyes.
Quickly searching for the rest, She piled them into the folder and ran out of the shuttle.
"Trixie we have to find her!" Ash commanded.
"Well yeah." Trixie retorted. "She won't last much..."
"Look!" Ash interrupted.
After receiving the folder, Trixie rapidly flicked through the files.
"What the hell is this?" She asked worriedly.

"Look familiar?" Ash replied.
They glanced at eachother, before Ash grabbed the folder and rolled it up, stuffing it down her vest.
She hopped on Trixie's saddle, putting her handlebars in a death grip.
"We need to find her." Ash commanded. "Now!"

Miranda's vision had gone blurry, the sun and heat viciously attacking her. Collapsed on the ground in pain, she weakly cried for help.
"Please..., anyone..."
As she began losing conciousnous, She could hear the faint sound of Trixie's motors in the distance.
With the last of her strength, she slowly lifted herself to her feet and raised her hands.
"THERE!" Ash called out in the distance.
As they raced towards her, she blacked out.

Chapter 18

A soft beeping filled the crisp, cold air.

"Miranda?" Ash asked softly.

She groaned weakly.

"You feeling alright?" Trixie asked.

"What...happened?" Miranda replied.

There was a silence.

"You got sun poisoning." Whittle said. "Worst case I've seen yet."

Miranda slowly flickered her eyes open, and sat up.

"You should stay down." Whittle commanded softly.

"Give her a second." Ash rebuttled.

As her vision returned, she could make out Ash and Trixie at the foot of her bed. Between them stood a tall, soft white, shapely gynoid. Her face was a black screen, with a pixelated mouth and eyes that seemed worried. Her forearms floated seperately from her body, slowly bobbing up and down. Protruding from the back of her head were two massive pig-tails, that hung below her waist.

Miranda stared for a moment, before looking around. To her right, Jace was sound asleep in another bed, a tube ran from his jaw up to a hovering, glass-like orb. To her left, the creature from before was snoring softly on a floor mat. It was covered in bandages, and had several tubes connected.

She then looked at her own arms, each had a tube connected.

"How are you feeling, Miranda?" Whittle asked.

"Sore." She groaned.

"I'm not surprised." Whittle quipped. "By the time we got you connected, your skin was half-baked, and you were almost desiccated."

"How long was I out?" She groaned again.

"A week and a half." Whittle replied.

"What?!" Miranda exclaimed.

She tried getting off the bed, before Whittle firmly pressed her back down.

The three of them had a short chuckle.

"A few hours, tops." Trixie reassured her.

Ash and Trixie glanced at eachother, as She pulled the folder from her vest. Trixie took a breath.

"We are very, truly.."

"Sorry." Ash interrupted. "For what happened."

There was a moment of silence as Miranda glared at them.

"It's...," She began. "It's alright. I would've done the same. I guess I should apologize too. I'm sorry, about the whole..., Whatever. I guess, I just..., lost control."

Ash sighed heavy, straightening the files.

"What are those?" Miranda asked.

Ash glanced at the folder, then back to Miranda.

"Are those my, files?" Miranda asked with a hint of anger.

"I found them in your shuttle," Ash began. "when we came looking for you."

Miranda grumbled softly.

"Whatever."

"We read the whole thing." Trixie started.

"And?" Miranda muttered.

"We can fix this!" Ash finished.

"Fix what?" Miranda grumbled again. "In case you forgot, I'm the one that..."

"Where did you get these, Miranda?" Ash interrupted.

"Why do you care?" She muttered again.

"Because half of those are based on our tech!" Whittle interjected.

The beeping of the monitor quickened, as Miranda's pupils dialated.

"We need to help eachother." Trixie started. "That technology is..."
"Whatever you're doing..." Whittle interrupted. "These idiots need to heal first. Now you two get out!"
She pointed to the door, staring at Trixie and Ash. They hesitated a moment, before trudging out.
"I know you're upset." Whittle started. "But you're not leaving until you're fully healed."
"How long?" Miranda grumbled.
"You'll be fully restored by tommorrow." Whittle replied. "Sleep tight."
As she tapped one her orbs, Miranda could feel a coldness spreading over her body, as her vision went blurry again. She quickly passed out.
Sometime later, Whittle caught up with Ash and Trixie in the ship's vehicle hangar.
"Would you guys mind telling me just what the hell is going on?"
"We're going for a ride." Ash coldly replied.

Chapter 19

A small gantry carried a wheeled vehicle over, and lowered it down in front of them. As the eight wheeled convertable touched the floor, the gantry retracted, and moved back into it's alcove.

As they climbed in, Ash started the vehicle.

The engine chugged softly then rapidly spooled up as the combustion cycle stabilized. Accent lighting flickered to life all around the car as the readout cluster began cycling diagnostics. The exhaust popped a few times as Ashlynn revved the engine, releasing a few small clouds of luminescent exhaust into the ship's hangar bay.

After putting the car in gear, the trio rolled down the hangar ramp and raced ahead toward the cave opening.

"What's this about, Ash?" Whittle asked annoyed.

"You tell me Whittle." Ash retorted softly.

"You're fucking with me, right?" She scoffed.

As they raced out into the night-time desert, Whittle hung over the side of the car waving her hand in the wind.

"You know what." She continued softly. "It doesn't matter."

Ash huffed in frustration and brought the car to a stop near a small oasis.

"No!" She stated coldly. "It does matter, Whittle."

"NO IT DOESN'T!" Whittle replied.

Ash and Trixie looked at her curiously.

"This all a dream, I'm still sleeping in the hangar." Whittle giggled sadly. "Damnit I miss you both so much!"

She began choking softly as tears animated down her face.

"I miss all of you."

Trixie placed a claw on her shoulder and spoke softly.
"Whittle..., this is real."
Whittle began wheezing as she stepped out of the car.
"Whittle are you okay?" Ashlynn worried.
The robotic girl collapsed on the edge of water. On her hands and
knees she began wheezing harder.
"N-no..." Whittle began sobbing.
Ash and Trixie moved closer as Whittle began crying into her hands.
Ashlynn placed a hand on one shoulder as Trixie placed her claw on
the other.
"Whittle..." Ash began softly. "We are here..., this is real..., we're ali..."
"NO YOU'RE NOT!" She screamed. "YOU'RE DEAD! YOU AND
TRIXIE! WE SAW YOU DIE!"
She stood to her feet and turned around. Her facial animations were
now a deep Crimson-Red.
"IT'S BEEN 5 YEARS!" Whittle shouted. "5 GODAMNED
YEARS! YOU ARE DEAD, AND THIS IS A DREAM! WHY
ARE YOU TORTURING ME LIKE THIS!?"
"Oh shit!" Trixie muttered.
"Whittle you need to calm down." Ash worriedly stated. "Please."
"NO!" Whittle screamed. "IT'S NOT FAIR."
"WHITTLE CALM DOWN!" Ash commanded.
"NO!" Whittle screamed again. "THIS IS IMPOSSIBLE, 5 YEARS
WE WATCHED YOU AND TRIXIE DIE!"
"Foxx!" Trixie began to worry.
"I know Trix." Ashlynn replied.
"YOU AND TRIXIE WERE SUCKED INTO A BLACK-HOLE!"
Whittle continued. "IT'S BEEN 5 YEARS! WE LOST HOPE, WE
GAVE UP, WE MOVED ON!"
Whittle began to stumble a bit as she lost her balance.
"Foxx!" Trixie restated. "She's..."
"Tracer shut up." Ashlynn commanded softly. "Whittle, please..."

"NO GODDAMNIT!" Whittle screamed. "EVERYONE MOVED ON, EVERYONE BUT ME AND RX. THIS ISN'T FAIR!"
She launched her forearm into the hood of the car with a violent screach then pulled it out of the fresh crater.
"I WANT TO WAKE UP." She continued. "JUST LET ME FUCKING WAKE UP AND FORGET ABOUT YOU!"
"GODDAMNIT WHITTLE!" Ashlynn shouted. "YOU ARE AWAKE! WE ARE ALIVE! NOW LET US EXPL..."
Trixie wrapped tail around Whittle.
"WHITTLE YOU NEED TO RELAX!" She screamed.
"JUST LET ME DIE ALREADY!" Whittle howled.
The wailing gynoid screached at a deafening tone before her eyes began turning a deeper shade of Red. With her eyes now a deep vibrant Red, she grunted, and scrunched herself tight.
"WHITTLE PLEASE, YOU NEED TO CALM DOWN!" Ash cried. "YOUR REACTOR IS GOING TO BURST!"
She scrunched herself tighter in Trixie's grip, as arcs of energy began leaping across her body, and along Trixie's tail.
"WHITTLE STOP, PLEASE!" Trixie cried.

Chapter 20

The arcs grew brighter as Whittle growled, her entire face glowing red, with warning symbols flashing all over.

"WHITTLE, PLEASE!" Ash and Trixie cried.

The arcing abruptly stopped, as Whittle vomited. Ash jumped out of the way, as an electrified stream of viscous liquid shot from her mouth, onto the hood of the car, rapidly dissolving it into a half melted puddle.

"SHIT, MY CAR!" She screamed. "DAMNIT WHITTLE!"

Trixie dropped her to the ground. As Whittle coughed and began to relax, Trixie looked over her tail for any signs of the corrosive fluid.

"YOU DESTROYED MY FUCKING CAR, WHITTLE!" Ash yelled. "IT'S REALLY US! FEEL BETTER?!"

Freaking out over her melted car, Ash cursed wildly, as she spit and kicked the dirt.

"That's the clearest sign you're getting." Trixie joked. "You know how much she loved that thing."

She placed her tail on Whittle's shoulder, as she chuckled with a sigh.

"Whittle," Trixie began. "We're sorry about what happened, but this is serious!

Whittle picked herself up and stumbled a bit.

"This doesn't make any sense." She groaned. "How is this possible?"

"It wasn't a black-hole." Trixie sighed. "It was some kind of new missle, it must have triggered our jump-drive. We were thrown across the universe. It fried our system and we crashed on Jacen's planet."

"Why..., Why didn't you contact us?" Whittle sniffled.

They looked over and saw Ash on her knees pounding the dirt, crying and cursing towards the sky.
"It's..." Trixie paused. "It's a long story."
"I built that from the ground up!" Ashlynn cried out. "And you destroyed it like that!"
Whittle stepped over to Ash and knelt down, placing a hand on her shoulder.
She only cried harder as she smacked Whittle's hand away, before scrunching into a ball.
"For fuck sake!" Whittle grumbled.
She lifted Ash by the shoulder and slapped her across the face.
"SNAP OUT OF IT!" She yelled. "It's just a damn car!"
Ash started growling at her, before Whittle slapped her again.
They stared daggers at eachother before Whittle embraced Ashlynn in a tight squeeze. Tears animating down her face again.
"I've missed you so much!" She wept softly.
Trixie rolled up behind them and placed her claw on Whittle's shoulder.
"We've missed you too, Murrcooni."
After a warm reunion, they all stepped back and took a breath.
"Sorry about your car, Ash." Whittle sighed.
Ashlynn chuckled softly.
"You're helping me fix it, don't forget that."
Whittle grumbled in defeat.
"Whatever, let's just get back to the ship."
"Alright." Trixie invited happily. "Hop on."
"I want to walk." Whittle replied.
"Suit yourself." Ash giggled.
Whittle a hand on both of them, with a sincere look.
"With you two."
"It's a two hour walk, at least." Ash said.

"We have plenty of time." Whittle replied. "Now let's start from the beginning."
Ash and Trixie glanced at eachother, then back to Whittle with a quiet huff.
"Alright, but you go first."

They sat near the oasis, rimenescing, and playing catch up.
The luke warm air rustled the lone tree, as the bio-luminescent water sparkled in tune with the stars.
"Remember the Startropics?" Ash sighed.
"I'll never forget." Trixie replied.
"Yeah," Whittle chuckled. "because that's when you learned you couldn't swim, Trix."
Trixie tapped her shoulder in response.
"Oh, you're funny." She taunted. "At least I didn't almost kill a group of Sea-foxes, Whittle."
"I didn't know I was allergic to rock-nuts." She defended.
"But you did know your reactor fluid is corrosive." Ash chuckled. "And still puked in the water."
"It's water soluble!" Whittle replied softly. "..., After five minutes."
"Well thankfully," Ash continued. "the little bastards were smart enough to swim away."
They chuckled softly, as they admired the stars.
"So what's the plan, Ash?" Whittle sighed.
"Phase one;" She started. "Get back to base, and start planning phase two. We need to get everyone on the same level again."
"You're gonna need a new plan then." Whittle sighed again.
"Why?" Trixie asked cautiously.
"I already told you guys." She whimpered. "Everyone split up after you disappeared."
"They're all still alive, aren't they?" Ashlynn worried. "We'll fnd 'em."

"Yeah, they're still alive." Whittle sighed.
She picked herself and began walking back torward the cave.
"Good luck finding them."

Chapter 21

The walk passed quickly, as Whittle filled them in about the others.
The night slowly faded into morning.
Jace and Miranda sat up tiredly in their beds, as Whittle released them from the tubes.
"Congradulations, you survived!" Whittle joked sarcastically.
"Where's Ash?" Miranda yawned.
"They're in the galley." Whittle replied.
"Oh boy." Jace said. "Breakfast!"
He winced and moaned, as his jaw popped back into place.
"Thomas will walk you there." Whittle added.
"Who?" They asked together.
"Wait in the hallway, he'll be around soon." Whittle said, shooing them out.
As they stepped into the hallway, Whittle shouted for Thomas.
"Thomas, wake the fuck up and show these idiots around!".
Before they could say anything, a voice replied with a yawn.
"Stop yelling, I'm awake. Where are they?"
"Med-bay." Whittle replied.
Seconds later, a holographic man flashed into existance outside the door.
He stood roughly six feet tall, with faint, but distinguishable wolf-like features. He wore a semiformal vest suit, with well groomed hair, and a small pair of bifocal glasses. A soft blue aura covered him.
He walked into the med-bay, with his tail flicking softly.
"Outside the med-bay." Whittle quipped.

He quickly stepped out, and locked eyes with Miranda, extending his paw-like hand.

"I'm Thomas." He said cautiously.

"Miranda." She replied, shaking it.

"And you are?" Thomas asked, moving his hand towards Jace.

"Jacen." He replied. "Call me Jace."

"Pleased to meet you both." He said, pulling away. "Follow me."

As they walked down the hall, Jace and Miranda couldn't help but look around.

"So where are we?" Miranda asked.

"You are on the Pegasus!" Thomas answered proudly.

"That name rings a bell." She pondered quietly.

"So there was a ship." Jace quipped.

"Is." Thomas replied. "There IS a ship."

"Sure, I guess." Jace sighed.

After a few hallways, and a flight of stairs, they stepped into a large room.

At one end was a large, holographic board, with strange markings and numbers, at the other end was a small kitchenette, where Ash and Trixie were talking.

"Look who finally woke up!" Ash joked, inviting them over.

"Yeah." Jace quipped. "Those sedatives really work."

"I meant Thomas." She chuckled.

"How was your nap?" Trixie added.

"Oh hah hah hah." Thomas replied sarcastically. "You're welcome by the way."

"Thank you Thomas." Miranda interjected.

"Oh..., You're welcome, Miranda." He replied with a curious tone.

After walking them over, He left with a spring in his step.

"Okay." Miranda started. "Let's talk."

Ash pulled the files from her vest, and spread them on the table.

"How did you get these scematics?" Ash questioned. "And from who?"

"Standard G.P.S procedure." Miranda replied.

"Don't be a smartass, Miranda" Ash quipped.

She paused for a moment, and relaxed with a sigh.

"Sorry." She replied. "Old habit, I guess."

"That's fair." Ash said.

"I got those files from an insider." Miranda sighed.

"Who?" Trixie asked.

Miranda fidgeted her hands for a moment.

"Are you going to kill them?" She asked nervously.

Ash and Trixie looked at eachother, then over to Jace, then back to her.

"Only if they try to kill us first." Ash replied.

"Alright." Miranda sighed. "She works final inspection, at the RyCat weapons facility on Nova Actual."

"Does she have a name?" Trixie quipped.

"Yeah..." Miranda sighed again. "Delta P. Phlanogin."

"PHLANGOGIN?!" Ash and Trixie exclaimed in unison.

"Yeah..." Miranda replied curiously."Why, You know her?"

Ash took a breath and sighed.

"Should've figured it would be that wackadoo nutjob."

"Wait, didn't we kick her out?" Trixie asked. "She had a kid right?"

Ash thought for a second.

"Whatever. Look, the point is she stole our tech. We need to know why."

They looked torwards Miranda.

"Did she say how she got them, or from where?"

Miranda cleared her throat.

"She contacted me out of the blue, talking about weapons being shipped across enemy borders."

"Enemy borders?" Ash wondered. "Where?"

"All over." Miranda replied curiously. "You know; Petria, Ona, Pan, Keteradonia and Tobyn Vega. The new skirmishes."

Ash and Trixie gasped, as they looked over the files again.

After a few minutes, they placed the papers on the table. Ash's face was now pale, and Trixie's eye's seemed highly worried.

"Hey Thomas?" Ash called out.

He appeared in a flash of pixels.

"Yes, what can I do ya for?"

"W-when...," Ash stuttered. "When did we disappear?"

He thought for a moment.

"You disappeared five and half years ago, near the planet Ona. Why?"

They all looked at eachother, as a strange tension grew in the air.

A smiled started forming on Miranda's face.

"Wait a minute..., That means you're..., y-you guys are..."

Miranda let out a squeal, before bursting into a full celebratory screech.

Ash, Trixie and Thomas worriedly glanced at eachother. Thomas fidgeted, dropping his ears with a huff.

"Well shit, this'll be interesting."

Chapter 22

After a moment of squealing and giggling excitedly, Ash planted Miranda back in her seat.

"You have no idea how excited I am!" Miranda giggled. "This is amazing!"

"Miranda, you need to calm down, Now." Ash demanded.

She struggled to keep herself still, as she nodded.

"We still need to figure out this weapon thing." Trixie added.

They sat looking over the files for a moment, when Miranda burst out giggling.

"I'm sorry, this is just too much. I have to ask, where's everybody else?"

Ash and Trixie sighed together.

"Well, uhm...," Ash struggled. "Look, Whittle knows more than us, ask her."

A defeated look came over Miranda's face, as she sighed.

"Sorry."

She stepped out of the chair and started walking away.

"HEY!" Ash demanded.

She jumped up and ran over to Miranda, grabbing her by the shoulder and planting her back at the table.

"Miranda this is your problem too, Remember?" Trixie reminded her.

She shook off the confusion.

"I'm sorry, It's just you guys are..."

"We aprpreciate the sentiment." Ash started. "But we have more pressing issues, Miranda."

After rearranging the files, Trixie started.

"First we need to find out what the weapons are for."

"We also need to figure out why Jace is involved." Ash continued.

"Wait a minute." He said. "Miranda, didn't you mention a super weapon?"

She thought for a second.

"Oh yeah, Hang on."

She grabbed the files off the table, and looked through them. After a moment she laid the files in order.

"Okay." She started. "This is all I know; all of these weapons have a specific target, and specialized design vectors..."

She pulled out a file.

"This one is Jace's amplifier, it's vectors are standardized."

They all examined it, passing around the file, until it came back to Miranda.

"Mass production?" Jace asked.

"That's what I thought too." Miranda replied. "But according to Delta, there's no production queue for it."

Ash grabbed the file.

"So what does that mean?"

Miranda grabbed the file back, and scoured it intensely.

"My best guess..., One device, multiple uses."

Ash grumbled.

"Beat would know."

Miranda perked up.

"Relax, Miranda." Ash sighed.

"HEY!" Whittle shouted. "GET BACK HERE!"

RX came galloping into the galley, as she passed the through the door, she tripped over herself and tumbled into the wall.

Whittle came sprinting over to her, and began searching for something.

After a moment, She pulled a needle like object from RX's lower stomach area, as she roared in pain.

"I TOLD YOU not run with these attached!" Whittle protested.
"You're lucky it didn't puncture anything!"
"A-HEM!" Ash said loudly.
Whittle and RX looked over. Whittle quickly slid the needle behind her back, with a fake cough.
"Oh shit, hey guys. What are you..."
"You two were supposed to be here half an hour ago!" Ash protested, crossing her arms.
"We are here now." RX chuckled.
"Just get over here!" Ash retorted. "This is important."
Whittle and RX trudged over with a sigh.

Chapter 23

After catching them up, and a discussion about proper medical ettiquete, they all relaxed in their seats.

"So let me get this straight." Whittle started. "That nutball Phlanogin stole our scematics? How?"

"That's what we're trying to figure out." Ash replied. "But most importantly, we..."

"DIGI-BIT!" Trixie exclaimed.

Everyone looked torwards her in confusion.

"The Pixel Digi-Bit convention!" She continued. "Delta always bragged about it!"

"And?" Whittle asked.

"If nothing else, That's where we can find her!"

"Trixie..." Ash began. "That's..., right! Trixie you're a genius!"

"Thomas!" She called.

Thomas came walking in, holding a plate a saucer.

"Yes?"

"Thomas I..." Ash paused.

Everyone curiusly looked at him as he took a sip.

"Well?" He asked.

"Anyway, We need to know everything about the Digi-Bit convention."

"I'll connect to the base and get started." He replied, disappearing.

Ash grabbed the files, and placed them back in her vest.

"Now what's the plan?" Whittle asked.

"Whittle, We're starting phase one!" Ash replied.

"Seriously?" She protested.

"And you still owe me a car, Murrcooni." Ash rebuttled.

Whittle grumbled in frustration.

"Oh for... Fine!" She said. "Come on RX!"

"Are we going for a run?" She asked excitedly, getting on all fours.

"Where are you going?" Ash asked sternly.

"To get your damn car." Whittle muttered.

She jumped onto RX, as she galloped down the hall.

"Should we follow them?" Trixie asked.

Ash glanced at her.

"Alright." She sighed. "Everybody on."

Within minutes, the three of them sped out of cave on Trixie, with a hover trailer in tow. They quickly caught up to RX.

Speeding out into the late day, they rode towards the setting sun, side by side.

"How far?" Miranda shouted over the wind.

"Past the oasis!" Trixie shouted back.

"There's an oasis out here?" Miranda shouted.

They laughed as they rode onward.

After some time, they pulled up to the melted car. Whittle and RX came skidding to a halt next to them.

"Is that the Terracruiser?!" Miranda asked excitedly.

She hopped off Trixie, and went running over, Ash quickly followed.

"The once and only." She replied sarcastically.

"What the hell happened to it?" Jace asked.

"I may have gotten too excited last-night." Whittle answered sheepishly.

"That was excitement?" He said in shock.

"Enough!" Ash interjected. "Let's get started."

They started dismantling the car piece by piece, placing them in the hover-trailer.

After sometime, the sun had set, and the trailer was full, with half of the car.

"I'll take this load back." Trixie said.
As she pulled away, RX took off running after her, laughing.
"Hey!" Whittle shouted. "Get your ass back here!"
RX was already out of earshot. Whittle quickly gave up and they all sat down to rest.
They quietly watched the stars.
"I have a question, Miranda." Jace said.
"Shoot buddy." She replied.
"Why were you excited back in the galley?" He asked curiously.
There was a moment of silence.
"Ash can I tell him?" Miranda asked excitedly.
"Sure." Ash sighed.
Miranda took a deep breath.
"Your, err..., our, friends here," She corrected herself. "are part of a massive band!"
"Okay." Jace said, confused. "Like, musicians?"
"An army of musicians." Miranda replied.
"I..., wouldn't say army." Whittle said.
"More like a..." Ash paused. "Pla-tune. Get it?"
They chuckled a bit.
"So you guys are a band." Jace said. "What instrument did you play, Ash?"
"Ash here is the second lead singer, and first guitarist." Miranda blurted.
Ash blushed.
"Second, lead singer?" Jace asked.
"It was a huge band." Miranda bragged.
"She's also our leader." Whittle quipped. "In case that wasn't very clearly obvious.
"Doesn't feel like it." Ash remarked sarcastically.
Miranda continued.

"They were conisdered heros by a lot of people, hundreds of billions if not more. Their performences united warring planets, reconnected factions and brought peace after the war."

"Whoa!" Jace exclaimed. "Seriously?"

"Seriously." Ash assured him.

"So what happened?" He asked. "Why did you guys, you know, split?"

"Well...," Ash replied. "It's kinda..."

She was interrupted by Trixie, squealing happily in the distance. As they all turned to look, Trixie was riding RX, who was dragging the trailer in her mouth.

"We'll tell you later." Ash finished.

Chapter 24

They finished dismantling the car, sending Trixie, RX and Whittle back with another load.

They sat to rest again, laying on the ground to stargaze.

"Beautiful, isn't it?" Ash sighed.

"Absolutely amazing!" Miranda replied.

"Sure is." Jace added.

They were quiet for a moment.

"So you guys just flew around space," Jace asked. "putting on shows and stuff?"

"Yeah." Ash replied softly.

"That's awesome!" He said quietly.

"Spectacular!" Miranda bragged.

Jace thought for a moment.

"Why didn't you guys ever play on Earth?" He asked.

"I figured you might ask." Ash sighed. "It's..., hard to explain."

She sat up.

"We're listening." Miranda said, sitting up as well.

"Alright." Ash cleared her throat.

"We..., were never on good terms with the G.P.S."

"Why?" Miranda asked.

"I figured you would know." Ash replied. "Do you not?"

"No?" Miranda replied.

"It's fine." Ash continued.

"Since the Milky-way galaxy is a G.P.S hotspot, we never wanted to risk it."

She took a breath.

"The Galactic Patrol Service didn't really like the fact we could just appear and perform. They couldn't do anything."
"Yeah." Miranda sighed. "They're a bunch of bureaucratic assholes."
Ash raised an eyebrow torwards her.
"Sorry." She sighed.
"The problem was," Ash continued. "neither could we."
"We didn't want to do anything, but anytime they gave us trouble, we had to restrain ourselves and let them finish their bitching."
They were silent as Ash took a breath.
"The reason I crashed landed on earth, was because they attacked first."
"Why?" Jace asked, now sitting up.
"Because they set us up." Ash sighed.
"We had just finished the show, and wanted to celebrate."
"The Rift reconnection!" Miranda exclaimed softly.
"Yeah." Ash replied.
"It was supposed to be our first show outside the Pan system. We wanted to celebrate, so me and Trixie grabbed some firework missles, and hopped in a shuttle."
"The one at the cave?" Miranda asked softly.
"Same one." Ash replied.
"Then what happened?" Jace asked curiously.
"Well," Ash continued. "we fired them off above the planet, putting on a little show. That's when the G.P.S came in."
Jace and Miranda inched closer in anticipation.
"As we fired the last one, a patrol shuttle flew across it's path, It was a direct hit. Within minutes, we were in a firefight, outnumbered six to one."
Jace and Miranda leaned in, paying close attention.
"They started firing on the Pegasus, so me and Trixie distracted them in the shuttle so it could get away."
They inched even closer.
"The next thing we knew, Trixie and I were falling to Earth."

"That was five years ago." She sighed.

The silence was broken, as the sound of Trixie's motors grew louder in the distance. They seemed to be laughing. A few seconds later, RX grunted as Trixie screamed excitedly. She bounced along the ground several times, rolling into a skid near Jace, Miranda and Ash.

A few seconds after, RX came padding to a halt near her, as Whittle jumped off into a sommersalt, landing in a superhero pose in front of the three.

"Man that was fun!" She proudly exclaimed. "I haven't laughed that hard since..., you guys alright?"

They quickly shook off their sadness.

"Erm, yeah." Ash cleared her throat. "Sorry. Just a lovely sky is all."

"Oh kay." Whittle said curiously. "Well, we dumped your car in the hangar."

"Oh man!" Trixie exclaimed. "You guys should have seen it, we had race battle on the way. I was winning!"

"Then RX decided to launch her." Whittle added.

She looked over as RX stood proud on all fours, giggling softly.

"So now what?" Trixie asked excitedly.

"Oh, uhh..." Ash thought.

"What about the shuttles?" Miranda asked.

"What about them?" Whittle answered.

"Can we fix those too?" Miranda asked again.

Ash sighed.

"Let's just get them on the ship first.

"Well come on then," Trixie began. "Let's get started."

They looked around at eachother curiously.

"Alright, fine." Whittle sighed.

Chapter 25

After checking for any loose pieces, they hopped on Trixie and rode off with RX and Whittle tailing once more.

RX quickly pulled along side them.

"Round 2!" Whittle shouted.

Before anyone could say anything, Trixie's tendrils sprouted.

"YOU'RE ON, BITCH!" She yelled back. "EVERYONE HOLD TIGHT!"

As she pulled ahead, RX galloped faster, keeping them equal.

"THIS IS AWESOME!" Miranda shouted.

"KICK HER ASS, TRIXIE!" Jace added.

Racing back to the cave, they taunted eachother with veering and drifting. Whittle launched her fist a few times, which Trixie blocked with her tail.

As Trixie pulled, ahead Whittle launched her fist again, accidently hitting Miranda.

"HEY!" She screamed.

"OH SHIT, SORRY!" Whittle shouted apologetically.

As her fist flew back, Miranda grabbed it and jumped across the speeding pair, Latching onto Whittle for support as she landed.

"You dropped this!" She taunted, holding Whittle's forearm.

"Sorry Miranda." Whittle apologised.

"Don't be." She replied. "NOW LET'S DROP THEM!"

She released Whittle's forearm as it floated back.

As she gripped Whittle's waist, Jace quickly scooted forward and gripped Ash's.

"RACE BATTLE!" Ash shouted, hunching forward.

Slowing down, Trixie flicked her tail at RX, as Whittle knocked it away with her fist. Strike after strike, they fought and taunted eachother. With the cave quickly came into view, they both sped up.
"FINAL STRETCH!" Trixie shouted.
Quickly approaching the shuttles, Trixie hopped into a drift, and slid to halt in front of the patchwork shuttle. Struggling to back pedal, RX slammed into the destroyed shuttle, sending Whittle and Miranda tumbling across the roof, and onto the ground in front.
"Oh shit!" The three chuckled.
Racing around to meet them, They saw Whittle searching for the rest of arms.
"AUGH!" Whittle shouted. "My freaking hands!"
As she wiggled her upper arms, they all burst out laughing. As Miranda picked herself up, Jace rushed over to help.
After brushing off, they caught their breath and looked around.
"Alright," Ash chuckled. "we need to give Whittle a hand finding her hands!"
As they started looking, RX came around the shuttle on her hind legs. She paused and twisted.
"Found them." She giggled.
Whittle's forearms were still clutching her shoulder fur.
They all broke out laughing again, as her forearms wiggled on their own. Whittle walked over, and lifted her upper arms into range, after a few seconds, her hands released their grip and floated back into place.
After another round of laughter, Ash gasped excitedly, running over to her shuttle.
"Let's just fly them in!" She yelled.
She climb in, Within seconds dust flurried underneath, as it lifted off the ground.
"No fuel!" Miranda shouted.
"No need!" Ash replied.

As one shuttle hovered over the other, She popped her head out of the hatch.

"Anybody got cables?" She teased.

Trixie looked over to RX and sighed.

"Would you mind giving me a hand RX?"

She nodded with a soft grunt.

After a few moments of explanation, RX and Trixie climbed onto the roof of the busted shuttle. Without hesitation, Trixie dug her tyre claws into the roof, as she drilled her tendrils into the bottom of Ash's craft.

"I'm connected!" Trixie exclaimed with hint of irritation.

RX quickly followed suit. Digging her foot claws around the edge of the new roof hole, She extened her arms around the bottom edges of the hovering craft, digging her fingers into the metal.

"Connected!" She roared softly.

"Get in you guys." Ash called out, pointing to the lower craft.

"This should be fun." Whittle quipped.

Miranda and Jace followed her inside, as Ash raised the shuttles.

Trixie and RX winced, as the shuttles pulled them tight.

"Hold on!" Ash called out.

"Just get it over with!" Trixie shouted angrily.

Within seconds, the lower shuttle lifted off the ground, and swayed softly as they moved forward.

After a few minutes of flying, the Pegasus came into view, as they pulled around the back.

Landing the craft as close as she could, Ash popped her head out again.

"One more thing." She yelled.

After Whittle, Jace and Miranda stepped away from the lower craft, Ash hovered the vessel into the vehicle bay, dragging the shuttle behind her, as Trixie and RX clung tight.

As soon as they came to a stop, Ash called out again.

"Okay, disconnect!"
Trixie and RX quickly removed themselves from the upper shuttle.
"Last time, Ash!" Trixie shouted.
As the craft landed nearby, Trixie and RX leapt off the roof and walked over to meet Ash, with Jace, Whittle and Miranda following close behind.
"Okay." Ash announced, stepping out. "We got my car, both shuttles, and everyone caught up. What next?"
"Sleep!" Whittle groaned. "That's next!"
As she walked away, RX looked at them for a moment before following along.
"You guys?" Ash questioned.
"I'm with them." Jace replied.
As he paced after them, Trixie rolled closer.
"I'm good for a few hours." Miranda sighed happily.
"I guess I'll join you." Trixie said.
"I was actually gonna catch some sleep too." Ash said awkwardly.
"That's fine." Trixie said. "I know my way around."
"Great." Ash said, pacing away. "See you in the morning!"
As she disappeared into the hallway, Trixie rolled over to the wall and hit a button. The door closed rapidly, pushing the shuttles farther in as it lifted into place.
"Now what?" Miranda asked.

Chapter 26

The next morning, Whittle and Jace sat around a table, eating their breakfast, while everybody else slept in.

Whittle swallowed her last bite with a grunt.

"So tell me about yourself, Jace."

"What do you want to know?" He replied, lowering his utensil.

"What do you do fun?" She asked.

"Well, uhh,...., I like listening to music." He answered. "I do art sometimes, too."

"Music, huh?" She quipped. "We make music you know. Well used to."

"Yeah." Jace said. "You guys kinda filled us in last night."

"Oh yeah." She gasped.

"So what did you play?" He asked curiously.

She paused for a moment, smiling at him.

"You ever hear of a Scratch Keytar?"

"A what?" He answered.

The smile grew wider.

"I'll show you." She said excitedly. "Hurry and finish eating."

Several minutes later, they were pacing down a hallway.

"You're gonna love this." She bragged softly.

"Probably." He said jokingly.

"No." She quickly rebuttled. "You'll love it. Trust me."

A few minutes later they stopped at a door.

"Give me a second." Whittle said.

After bringing up a keypad, she entered a code, and the door opened slowly. As they stepped inside, the lights flickered on by themselves, revealing a studio of some kind.

Familiar and strange instruments were sitting in their stands, there were cords spread all across the floor. Whittle stepped over to a guitar-looking instrument, that had 2 disks on the body and several buttons running up the neck. She picked it up, and placed the strap around her chest, as Jace sat on a nearby couch.
"This, is a scratch keytar." She said, flipping a switch on the bottom. As the amplifiers came alive, Whittle slowly turned the disks one by one.
"It's mostly an accessory instrument." She explained. "But here's a sample anyway."
Slowly spinning the disks, she produced a hybrid electronic/ funky beat as sound flowed from the amps.
Jace could feel the music as it danced through his body, titilating his nerves.
After several minutes, Whittle faded out and lowered the instrument.
"So?" She asked. "Did you love it?"
At a loss for words, he simply gave her a thumbs up.
After placing the instrument back on the stand, She walked over to the couch and relaxed. Splaying her arms and legs loosely.
"You know." He said curiously. "You're very human-like for a robot."
"Because I am human." She sighed. "Atleast I used to be."
She leaned forward and twitched her toes.
Jace perked up in curiousity, leaning in close, watching as her toes floated and danced around the bottom of her legs.
"What happened?" He asked.
"It's messed up." She replied. "You don't want to hear it."
"Yes I do." He said. "It can't be that bad."
She looked at him, her eyes seemed to be tearing up, as pixels bubbled near the bottom, her mouth quivering.
"I'm sorry." Jace quickly apologized. "I didn't mean to..."
"Its alright," Whittle sighed. "I guess I've been through worse."
There was a moment of silence.

"You wanna talk about it?" He asked. "If not it's cool, I mean, err...
sorry."
"Sure." She sighed again. "Just..., sure."
She took a deep breath.
"How old do you think I am, Jace?" Whittle sighed.
"I uh, 20?" He replied sheepishly.
"116." She said.
"What?" He asked in surprise.
"I'm 116." Whittle replied.
"Wow uh..., you look good." He said.
"I've been a synth for almost 100 years." She sighed.
"Damn." He said.
"It get's worse." She sighed.

Chapter 27

"After we relocated," Whittle continued. "We did our best to try and get used to it."

"Okay." Jace said.

"After a month or so," She continued. "Keen and I started to explore a little bit."

Jace kept listening intently.

"There had been reports of children disappearing, they told us it was the monsters outside the wall."

Jace was almost off the seat, as he scrunched in anticipation.

"But me and my baby brother, being the "super awesome explorers" we were, decided to fight monsters and save the kids. So, we started exploring near the city wall and found a huge fracture. I wanted to tell guards, but Keen wanted to be a little glory-hound, and took off running through it."

The pixelilated tears began forming again, as she continued with a soft chuckle.

"We found ourselves in huge, grassy field, Keen was so excited I thought he would explode, he thought we were in another world!"

Whittle started crying softly, Jace wanted to comfort her, but didn't want to interrupt.

After a few seconds, she caught her breath.

"Well, for a few minutes, we were. The grass was soft, the air was fresh, and the sun was just beginning to set. I almost forgot why we left the city, but Keen didn't. We walked until the city disappeared behind us, and the sun had long since gone down. By this time it had gotten a

little colder, so Keen and I started a small fire, and that's when the real monsters appeared."
She squeaked and began crying a little harder, tears were animating down her face quickly, bouncing along the bottom sides. Jace carefully placed an arm around her shoulder.
"Hey, Whittle, look I..." Jace comforted her. "I didn't mean to..."
"We didn't know what hit us." She choked.
"We woke up strapped to these cold, hard tables. The last thing I remember before blacking out, was Keen screaming."
Whittle began crying harder, cupping her face-screen as Jace comforted her.
"That was the last time I ever saw him."
She let loose and wailed bitterly. Jace pulled her close, squeezing her softly, sliently comforting her as she cried.
After a few minutes, she caught her breath.
"When I woke up, the first thing I saw was Ash rummaging through a pile of garbage. I couldn't feel my limbs, so I called for help. She came over and stared at me."
Whittle chuckled softly.
"Want to know the first thing she said?"
Jace nodded.
"Wow! You can talk?!"
She continued with a sigh.
"She was always a weird bitch."
"So...," Jace spoke carefully. "is this your first body?"
"No." She replied softly.
Without another word, she got up and walked over to a drawer. A few seconds later she sat back down with a picture frame.
"This was." Whittle sighed, handing it over.
The frame held a paper image, which depicted a strange looking, younger, scruffier Ash. Resting on her head, was a beachball sized orb,

with a single, large blue eye in the center. It had a shutter covering the bottom half, as if it were smiling.

"Cute." Jace said instinctivly. "Err, I mean..., sorry."

"It's fine." Whittle chuckled softly. "That was 20 years ago."

"Whoa." Jace said. "Wait, but that means you..."

"80 years." She sighed. "I was asleep for 80 years."

"Damn." He exclaimed softly.

"Yeah..." She sighed again.

There was a moment of silence.

"So when did you get this body?" He asked.

"18 years ago." Whittle replied. "For 2 years I floated beside Ash, until she scrapped a platoon of drones and some busted screens to give me this body."

"That's..., nice of her." Jace said curiously.

"Yeah..." Whittle sighed. "She said she would find a way to get me an organic body."

"That's pretty cool." Jace said with a hint excitement.

"7 years ago." She quipped softly.

"Oh." Jace sighed.

There was a moment of silence as they looked around the room.

"Can I...," Whittle started. "Ask you a weird question?"

"Go ahead." Jace replied happily.

Chapter 28

"Okay...," She sighed nervously. "Do you..., like synths, err..., robots?"
"I think they're pretty damn cool!" He exclaimed softly.
She chuckled a bit.
"N-no, I mean...," Whittle continued sheepishly. "Do you think,
they're, uh..., attractive?"
Jace blushed a little.
"Well," He cleared his throat. "I mean, erm, ..., Yeah."
Two small, pink dots appeared on Whittle's cheek areas.
"Really?" She asked with a hint of excitement.
Jace chuckled with a bit of anxiety.
"Well, don't tell..."
He was interrupted, as Whittle softly but quickly pressed her face into
his. A few small sparks jumped between his lips and her mouth
animation, before she pulled away.
The pink dots seemed larger now.
"I-I'm sorry it's just...," She hesitated. "Look I know this is weird but...,"
"Whittle..." He exclaimed softly.
"I'm still a virgin." Whittle squeaked.
"Do that again." Jace said with a smile.
"Really?" She asked excitedly.
He simply nodded.
She scooted closer and leaned into his face, her eyes appeared to close
as her mouth made a kissing shape. Jace leaned in aswell, slowly
making contact with her screen matieral. As his mouth touched hers,
tiny sparks began dancing around his lips. After a few seconds,
Whittle instinctivly pushed Jace onto the couch, keeping in contact.

Jace felt himself getting aroused, as a soft heat began warming his crotch. A few seconds later, the heat spiked, becoming painful. He pushed her off slowly as the heat faded.

Checking his groin, he quickly noticed Whittle's pubic area was glowing red, as the pink dots on her face doubled in size.

"W-Whittle, are you...," He asked curiously. "getting turned on?"

She nervously looked down at herself, then quickly back to him.

"I-I..., uh..., Jace look I...," Whittle stuttered nervously.

"That's so...," He paused. "Hot!"

Whittle quivered as her crotch and the pink dots softly grew brighter. She quickly pinned him down again, pressing her face into his, sending more sparks dancing across his lips.

As the sparks increased, Jace could motion on his pants, as Whittle pressed herself closer. The motion got deeper as he realized she was dry humping him.

The heat seemed to fade, as Whittle rubbed a little harder with a frustrated moan, causing Jace to pull her closer.

After several passionate moments, she pulled away with a soft gasp, looking down at her crotch with another frustrated moan.

"Whittle." Jace cooed. "That was amazing."

"Stupid genderless chassis." She grumbled.

"Are you okay?" He asked softly.

"Jace, I...," She quivered. "think I...,"

She paused for a moment.

"It's not fair." She sighed.

"What?" He asked worriedly.

"I finally found someone who likes me...," She muttered. "and I..., can't even get laid."

The glowing from her cheeks and crotch slowly faded.

"Whittle, look." Jace reassured. "I loved it, really."

"I know." She replied sadly. "I did too, but this stupid chassis..."

They were silent for a moment.

"Can you do me a favor?" Whittle asked confidently.

"Yes!" He replied

"When I finally get an organic body..." She paused. "Will you be my first?"

Jace gasped excitedly.

"Absolutley!" He smiled.

Whittle smiled back, as she leaned onto his shoulder.

They braced eachother for a moment.

"One more thing." She added.

"Sure." Jace replied.

She started with a huff.

"Nobody. Not Ash, not Miranda, not even Trixie, not a single person, can know about this."

"Why?" He asked.

She continued.

"Because if Ash finds out, she'll kill us."

Chapter 29

After cuddling for a moment, Jace perked up.

"What about Thomas?" He asked worriedly.

"What about him?" Whittle answered.

"Isn't he..., like, everywhere on the ship?"

"Me and Thomas have an agreement." She replied. "Plus, he's a lazy dick."

Jace pondered for a second.

"What does that..."

"It means," Whittle interrupted. "That he's only "around" whenever someone calls him. Thomas stays on the bridge until then."

"Oh, okay." Jace said in relief.

After a few more minutes of cuddling, Whittle stood to her feet.

"Okay, look." She started. "No kissy-kissy, no cuddling, no grab-assing, Just.., nothing romantic around them, alright?"

"Strictly professional?" Jace answered.

"You got it!" Whittle replied confidently. "They'll be up any minute now, I was just showing you the instruments, because you asked. Yes?"

"They're very cool." Jace replied in tone. "Thanks for the demo."

"Thanks for asking." Whittle replied. "It's been a while since I played."

They paused for a moment to smile in agreement.

"Anyway," She continued. "Let's see if they're up yet."

After one last peck, Whittle shut down the studio and led Jace back up the hallway.

Trixie yawned, as she rolled into the galley.

"Morning bedhead." She said to Ash. "Where's Whittle?"

Ash grunted as she took a sip of her drink.

"Fair enough." Trixie replied.

After using the food maker, she carried her plate over, and sat across from Ash.

Her lower jaw squeaked open, revealing several tiny cutters. She quickly dumped the food in, as she snapped her jaw shut. Faint buzzing could be heard, as she rolled back to the food maker.

A few moments later, Whittle and Jace came walking in.

"Thanks again for the tour." He said.

"Just stay away from Ash's car." Whittle replied. "She get's really, Oh hey guys."

"Whittle!" Trixie gasped happily. "Good morning!"

"Good morning Trixie." Whittle replied. "Morning Ash!"

Ash grunted again, sipping her drink.

"Long night huh?" She continued.

"Alright, I give." Ash groaned. "Good morning. Happy?"

"Yes." Whittle replied teasingly.

As she and Jace took a seat, Trixie dumped the contents of another plate into her jagged maw, Grunting happliy as the buzzing started again.

"Ah, I've dying to taste that again."

"Miranda still sleeping?" Whittle asked.

"Poor thing is passed out in Zik's room." Trixie replied. "She wanted to test the bed and just, out."

Whittle chuckled.

"Zik's going to be pissed when she finds out."

Jace stared at Trixie, with a mix of confusion and interest.

"I forgot you could do that."

"So did I." She replied.

Chapter 30

After finishing their breakfast, they relaxed.

"So now what?" Jace wondered.

"Now, we get back to base." Ash replied.

Whittle and Trixie perked up. They looked over with a mix of worry and excitement.

"About time." Whittle quipped. "Let's go."

She stood to stretch, with a relaxed grunt.

"Wait, now?" Trixie asked.

"Yes. Right now." Whittle replied. "Let's get going Ash."

Everyone quietly looked torwards her.

"Do we have enough power?" She asked lazily.

"THOMAS!" Whittle shouted.

Thomas flashed in at the door.

"Guys, you need to see this."

A holographic screen appeared on the wall at the back of the room. Two news anchors frantically scrambled things on their desk, as a ticker ran across the bottom, displaying the words: "breaking news!"

"In possibly related news," The male started. "The Galactic Patrol has put out an alert for one Miranda Rachel Briggswelle, Chief Intellignce Officer for the G.P.S. She is wanted for questioning about the attack on the Maroon. Interplantery authorities are offering a reward for information on her whereabouts. Captain Salazar P. Mordis has this to say:

"Officer Briggswelle took off in a stolen shuttle during the attack."

A video popped up, showing Miranda and Jace running through the hangar, hopping in the shuttle and blowing the hangar doors off.

"She disabled the onboard trackers." Captain Mordis conitnued. "So I'm offering a king's bounty to anyone that is able to detain her, and bring her to The Maroon. Use extreme caution when doing so, Officer Briggswelle has G.P.S Defence training, is armed, and is extremely dangerous."

The video disappeared, as the female started.

"Captain Mordis has declined information about Officer Briggswelle's partner, only claiming he will double the bounty for whomever detains them both."

As the screen went blank, they all looked towards Jace, with a look of intense shock.

"Thomas when was this broadcasted?" Ash demanded.

"That was live!" He replied.

"Oh crap!" Trixie sighed.

"Holy shit!" Whittle exclaimed.

Ash frantically looked around.

"Alright, Let's get this hunk of shit moving. NOW!"

Everyone scattered, checking around the ship and cave for anything missing. After a good moment, the hatches locked into place as they gathered on the bridge.

"Get us out of here, Thomas!" Ash commanded.

The view screen pixelated open, revealing the darkened cave outside. With the flip of a lever, lights flickered on outside the ship, lighting up the cave.

"Thomas." Ash called softly. "Check for malfunctions, all systems. Show the results on view."

"Give me a second." He replied.

'Now Thomas!" She commanded.

The lights on the bridge pulsated for a moment, before readouts appeared on the viewscreen.

"Double checked, all clear." Thomas said confidently. "Atmospheric compensation complete in 5 minutes."

"Great." Ash exclaimed.

"Now let's get the hell outta here!" Whittle added.

The ship rattled and shook, as power began flowing to the thrusters.

"You all might want to grab a seat." Ash warned.

The power readout slowly filled, as the Pegasus shook a little more, the cave outside now vibrating, as everyone strapped into a seat.

As the readout passed halfway, another popped up.

"Atmospheric compensation complete." Thomas said. "Beginning gravity recalibration!"

Loose items around the bridge began levitating wildly, everyone started floating in their seats.

"This is awesome." Jace exclaimed.

"Not for long." Whittle sighed.

The ship rattled as the cave outside began moving sideways.

Chapter 31

Everyone started sinking into their seats, as the items fell. The cave was now moving faster, with Ash gripping the control yoke tight. As the second readout filled, every felt relief as gravity returned to normal.

"Gravity recalibration comeplete." Thomas said. "Beginning toxin..."

"THOMAS!" Ash, Trixie and Whittle, screamed in unison.

"Kidding!" Thomas quickly rebuttled. "Just kidding. Beginning power cycle."

The viewscreen flickered, as the cave entrance moved into sight. With the second readout quickly filling, the first finished loading.

"Power has been cycled." Thomas said confidently. "All systems are go."

"So are we!" Ash exclaimed.

As she opened throttle, The cave entrance grew larger, and faster on the viewscreen. Seconds later, the Pegasus shot out of the cave, Skimming along the desert floor.

"I'm not gonna lie." Whittle said. "I'll miss this place."

Ash grunted as she moved the yoke.

"What the hell?!" She exclaimed.

"What?" Trixie asked worriedly.

"I've lost control." Ash replied.

"Fault on the forward lift thrusters." Thomas said.

A model of the ship appeared on screen, with a warning near the damage.

"I,m on it!" Trixie shouted, racing off the bridge.

Seconds later, another warning appeared on the model, showing a hatch open. Before anyone could say anything, scratching could be heard moving down the hull. After a few minutes, the first warning disappeared, leaving only the hatch, which disappeared shortly after, as Trixie came racing onto the bridge.

"We told you to check all systems!" Trixie huffed. "Jackass!"

As she reconnected her belt, Ash grunted again, angling the ship skyward.

"Hold on!" She commanded.

Snapping the yoke to the right, she rolled the ship several times, before leveling out.

"What the hell was that?!" Whittle exclaimed.

"Just making sure." Ash replied.

The sky faded into open space, as they shot into the stars. Everyone sighed in relief.

"So how long, Ash?" Jace asked.

"A few hours." She replied. "Thomas, charge the drive."

"Actually..." He replied sheepishly. "The drive may... be busted."

"What was that?" Ash questioned sternly.

Chapter 32

After several minutes of viciously berating the disembodied voice, and smashing things against the wall, Ash finally settled down.

"Do I make myself VERY clear?!" She huffed.

"Y-yes ma'am." Thomas stuttered. "Won't happen again."

"Now get started!" Ash commanded.

"Yes ma'am." Thomas repeated.

The lights flickered, as several meters appeared on screen.

Everyone watched her fearfully, silently waiting for something else.

"While Thomas is running A FULL SYSTEM SCAN!" Ash yelled.

"We should be on alert. Start searching the ship for weapons."

"I got the hangar." Trixie said hastily.

She squealed her tires, and took off down the hall.

"I'll get the med-bay." Whittle added.

She skittered to the door, and bolted after Trixie.

"Jace." Ash began. "Find Miranda, fill her in and get to the war room.

See if she can give us attack patterns for the Maroon."

As he took off, She spoke again.

"RX should be in her room, it's across from Zik's. Wake her up and send her to the hangar."

Jace hesitated for a moment.

"Jace GO!" She commnded.

He bolted off.

After a moment, He came skipping to a halt in front of a Black and Orange door. With a soft knock, it split down the middle and flashed open.

As he sprinted inside, Jace slipped on Miranda's uniform with a shout.

"Miranda, WaHHT THE FU..."
As he landed with a thump, She bolted up tiredly, forming a gun shape
with her hands. With her eyes half closed, she looked around the
room frantically, as she yawned.
"Freeze!"
Jace picked himself up with a grunt.
"Miranda, get up now!"
"Oh, hey Jace." She yawned again. "What's up?"
"I think your captain found us!"
"Oh, that's cool." She replied. "Tell him I need..., FUCK!"
She ripped the blankets away, and hopped off the the bed.
Jace blushed as she moved around the room. Her head was covered
with fuzzy bed hair, she wore only a pink bra with blue panties.
He could see faded, symmetric scars, lining the fair skin around her
ribs. He felt his blood racing.
Seconds later, She grabbed her pants and shoes, racing through the
door.
"JACE COME ON!"
He shook it off and went after her, pausing immedietly.
"Hang on!" He shouted.
Running to the door across the hall, he gave it a few hard knocks.
After a moment, a loud roar could be heard.
"WHAT!?"
"RX, we're under attack!" Jace replied.
"WHAT?" RX asked.
Loud thumping grew closer. Thinking fast, Jace hopped out of the way,
right as She burst through the door and skid to a halt.
"WHERE?" She asked.
"Hangar!" Jace replied.
Without another word, she went galloping down the hall at full pace.
"Okay, let's go." Jace commanded.

Chapter 33

"How are we looking Trix?" Ash asked.

"Almost done on this side. She replied.

"Same here." Ash continued. "Let's hurry and get this..."

She was interrupted, as RX came galloping into the hangar. With a grunt she leapt over the catwalk railing and tumbled near Trixie and Ash.

"ATTACK! WHERE?" She asked.

Ash and Trixie glanced at eachother.

"We need to get this Jump drive back in place." Ash began. "Then we can tell you."

Without another word, RX grabbed the massive pair of cylinders, and hefted them over her head.

"Hold it there!" Trixie demanded.

They ran their tools over the drive, securing it in place. After reconnecting a few wires, they hopped off the platform.

"Okay, follow us!" Ash said.

They sprinted up the hall, stopping at the med-bay.

"Whittle!" Trixie called out. "Get to the war room!"

"Right behind you!" She replied.

As they took off, Whittle skipped out out of the med-bay, and sprinted after them.

"Thomas, how are we doing?" Ash demanded.

"The drive is syncronized and charging." He replied.

"Good." She continued. "Take over the console and wait for my signal."

The lights flickered as they rounded the corner.

After a moment or two, they all came skipping to a halt in the war room. Miranda stood shirtless on the other side of the table, her hair in a mess.

A hologram floated in the center, showing a live model of the Pegasus.

Jace came running over to her with some papers.

Screens on the back wall danced with models of ships and planets.

Miranda looked up.

"You guys should know, Your system is easier to work than the G.P.S training simulator."

After everyone took a seat, Miranda filled them in, rotating the hologram, as she brought a missle close to the ship.

"The missle would impact here, crippling the thrusters. That's when he..."

"Okay hang on." Ash interrupted. "Let's get this clear; The G.P.S Maroon is carrying warp-killer missles, and taggers?!"

"Yes." Miranda sighed.

"What the hell happened in the past five years?" Trixie asked.

"Don't ask me." Whittle quipped. "We've been in that cave for most of them."

Ash and Trixie glanced at her.

"Why?"

"I'm the medic, remember." She continued. "You guys never tought me how to fly this thing."

"Oh bullshit Whittle." Ash scoffed. "How did you get it in there?"

"Thomas crashed." RX replied. "Autopilot failure."

A soft shaking could be felt all round the room.

Ash sighed deep, standing from her chair.

"Just can't catch a break."

She bolted out the room.

Chapter 34

After regaining control of the ship, Ash called everyone to the bridge.
As they filed in and took their seats, She gave them a briefing.
"Alright look. The G.P.S is looking for Miranda, and Jace."
She pointed to them before continuing.
"Delta stole our tech scematics, our team is broken and we're running bare bones at the moment."
Everybody nodded in agreement.
"Thankfully, no-one is looking for The Pegasus. And hopefully, The terra-base is still intact. So we'll began there, and plan as we go."
Everybody nodded again.
"We managed to rig the drive, it should be safe for a jump."
"Should be?" Whittle asked.
"You know how this works, Whittle." Ash replied. "Just strap in and hold tight."
With an annoyed sighed, she brought the restraints across her body and secured them tight.
"You too guys." Ash continued.
Everyone else did the same, as Ash took a seat at the control console.
With press of some buttons, energy started building up on the hull, before everyone was sucked into their seat. A tunnel of swirling, mutli-chromatic light danced on the viewscreen.
After several hours, the Pegasus jumped out of sub-space. A planet grew in the distance.
"Okay." Ash began." We'll be home in a few minutes. Everybody go ahead and relax."

With a sigh of relief, Everyone except Ash sorely pulled themselves from their seat.

"Thomas, let Ana know we're coming in." Ash commanded.

There was no response.

"Thomas!" She repeated.

A strip of lighting flickered and popped, sending a shower of sparks across the bridge.

"THOMAS, RESPOND!" Ash repeated frantically.

Several warnings appeared on the view screen, as the ship began rocking. As the entered the atmosphere, flames danced across the hull. Several alarms went off as more warnings appeared.

"SOMONE GET ANA ON THE LINE, NOW!" Ash screamed.

Everyone quickly buckled themselves in. Whittle's face started showing connection symbols, as Trixie's eyes flashed and flickered different colors.

The ship rocked and shook violently, as they leveled out near the ground.

"PLEASE TELL ME WE HAVE A RESPONSE!" Ash yelled.

"NOTHING!" Whittle and Trixie screamed in unison.

As a mountain range came into view, Ash fought the yoke for control. The ship dropped lower until it began scraping the ground. Screaching and tearing filled the bridge at deafening levels.

With the mountain range growing closer, a hangar could be seen near the bottom. As the ship bounced along the ground, it got larger, becoming a massive wall of metal.

"EVERYBODY, HANG ON!" Ash yelled.

She started slamming levers down, as the control console sparked. Snapping the yoke to left, She brought the ship starboard side to the hangar door, as they slid to halt.

After a few minutes of recovery, everybody removed themselves from their seat, and wobbled about the bridge. Lights flickered, as warnings continued to flash across the cracked screen.

Ash muttered as she undid her restraints.

"He better not be dead, because I want to kill him myself.

She wobbled down the hall, as everyone continued to catch their breath.

Chapter 35

"Oh shit, this is bad!" Ash muttered.

The terminal core sparked wildly, as it flickered and faded. Bits and pieces lay scattered around the room. A small fire danced in the corner.

Ash smacked the core a few times, trying to keep Thomas alive inside. "Hey, stay with me Thomas." She commanded softly. "We made it, let's get you inside."

The core seemed to flicker in agreement.

"Hang on buddy." Ash sighed.

"SHIT! SHIT! SHIT!" Whittle screamed down the hall. "ASH WHERE THE HELL ARE YOU!?"

"WHAT IT IS!?" She screamed back.

"ASH WE NEED TO GO NOW!" Whittle replied. "THE COILS RUPTURED, THE SHIP'S ABOUT THE BLOW!"

"FUCK!" She yelled.

Thinking fast, She grabbed a small cube from the center of the core, and bolted to the door. As she came through, Whittle snagged her arm and dragged her the other way.

"This way genius!"

"Where's everyone else?" Ash worried.

"Outside, now run damnit!" Whittle replied.

After a tense moment, They came speeding out the hatch. RX was waiting on all fours. Clutching tighter, Whittle jumped, carrying Ash and herself onto RX's back, as she took off galloping along the moutain range.

"WHERE ARE THE OTHERS?" Ash worried again.

"TRIXIE'S GOT 'EM." Whittle replied. "HOLD THIS!"
She handed Miranda's rucksack to Ash, and clutched RX's fur tighter as she picked up speed.
Seconds later, a bright flash of light surrounded them. In the blink of an eye, RX reached around, Grabbing them off her back and clutching them tight, as a deafening gust of wind launched them farther ahead.
After tumbling and bouncing in to a patch of grass, RX released her grip, letting Ash and Whittle slid to the ground.
After a while, Ash's eyes flickered open. Everyone stood around her, worried but thankful.
She groaned sorely.
"Please tell me that was a dream."
Trixie sighed.
"Well..., the good news is, we saved Thomas and the files."
"What's the bad news?" Ash sighed.
"The Pegasus, and everything on it, was destoyed." Whittle answered quietly.
"Goddamnit." Ash choked.
"There's more." Trixie continued. "The explosion tripped security. All the main guns are online, no doubt the security field is active."
"Any reponse from Ana?" Ash sighed.
"Still nothing." Whittle answered.
"Fucking kill me." Ash choked.
Whittle offered a hand, after pulling Ash to her feet, she brushed her off.
"I'm gonna talk a walk." Ash began. "Let me know when you think of something."
She walked off with a heavy sigh. Everyone retreated into the nearby forest. After several hours, the sun began to go down. Everyone sat around a small fire, eating berries.
Curious, Miranda watched as Whittle and Trixie popped the berries into their mouths, Closely eyeing them as Whittle formed a circle

with her mouth animation, and slid berries into the black screen seemlessly.

"Okay." She started. "I have to ask, How can you guys eat if you're robots?"

Everyone glanced at her. Trixie and Whittle glanced at eachother, then back over.

"Seriously?" Whittle replied.

Miranda simply nodded.

Trixie went first with a sigh.

"I have a cruch-cutter system connected to a morph-matter bio-reactor."

"Oh, Okay." Miranda sighed. "What about you, Whittle?"

"Goddamnit." She grumbled. "The lower half of my screen made of transmorphic phase-matter. It's connected to a multi-state bio-plasma conversion system. Happy?"

"Mm-hmm." Miranda replied.

After a few moments, Miranda sighed again.

"So can you guys use the bathroom?"

Trixie and Whittle spit the berries from their mouths in shock!

"MIRANDA!"

Chapter 36

They sat for a while, quietly watching the fire dance. Ash could still be
heard cursing, and weeping bitterly in the far distance.
"I've never seen her like this." Trixie sighed.
Whittle scoffed.
"This is nothing. Try watching her tear a shuttle to pieces.
Barehanded."
"Why though?" Miranda asked.
"She thought they were trying to capture us." Whittle continued. "She
dove through the viewscreen, and tore it apart from the inside. That
was the first time I've seen her risk her life for me..., The only time
actually."
"Yeah." Trixie sighed. "If only she could tear into the base and...,
THAT'S IT!"
She activated her lights and took off into the forest.
"I'LL BE RIGHT BACK!"
"Don't wait up for us." Whittle quipped sarcastically.
They sat for sometime, watching the fire slowly fade.
"This is pretty nice actually." Miranda said. "Quiet, natural, fresh, No
jackass captain screaming at you every five minutes."
Whittle chuckled, popping another berry into her mouth.
"Try having Ash for a captain."
Miranda perked up.
"If you thought your captain was bad, I feel sorry. You ever have to
replace someone's entire spine after a training session?"
A subtle look of fear came over Miranda's face.
"I have, twice." She paused. "Mine."

"Damn." Jace exclaimed softly.

"She just gets so intense." Whittle continued. "At one time, we had to barricade ourselves in the galley, when a band of pirates broke into the base."

"For real?" Miranda asked.

"Oh yeah." Whittle continued. "It was so bad, one of them even begged us to let her past. I felt bad about it, But I sure as hell wasn't taking her place."

"Damn." Miranda started. "She must really care about you guys. Taking on a band of pirates like that, alone."

"Oh no." Whittle chuckled. "She's a glory hound, through and through. Don't get me wrong, we all have our faults. But hers are..., unique."

Jace giggled.

"Anybody ever try to touch her ears?"

Whittle burst out laughing, bits and peices of berry flying off her face. "Did you?"

"One poke." Jace continued. "One little poke on the back..., And she goes ballistic. I thought Trixie would die before I did. She held her back, trying to calm her down as I apologized."

They chuckled for a moment.

"Jace I gotta say." Whittle started. "I don't know what you did, but Ash seems to have calmed down a lot!"

"I wish I knew." He giggled.

They went silent again. As the fire began dying, Whittle tossed on another log. RX snored nearby.

"So what kind of robot are you?" Miranda asked.

Whittle grumbled with an annoyed sigh.

"You ask a lot of questions, Miranda. Where you always this talkitive?"

Miranda sighed deep.

"I'm sorry. It's just..., I was you guys' biggest fan as a kid. I listened to all your music. I begged my dad to take me to your shows, but he would always say; "No, It's too dangerous. You can watch them from home."
She took a breath.

"And now, I'm sitting around a campfire, next to Whittle Murrcooni and RX. Two star members of KatsKan; The greatest band in the universe. You guys were heros to a lot of people..., you were my heros."
Tears started rolling down her cheek.

"I had a feeling Ash and Trixie weren't dead. Everyday in bootcamp, even afterwards, I would tell myself; "Once I get out, I'm going find them and reunite the the band!"
She started crying softly.

"But I gave up a few years ago. I felt terrible. I didn't want to, but...,"
She wept a little harder. Whittle and Jace glance at eachother worriedly. RX came walking around the fire, and placed a massive hand on her shoulder.

"Do not cry." She smiled.
After wiping away tears, She continued.

"I have you to thank, Jace."
He blushed, placing a hand on her other shoulder.

"Thank you."
Miranda sighed.

"And I guess Delta too, turns out that idiot step-sister of mine was good for something after all."
They all sighed happily and relaxed.
After a moment, Whittle's eyes grew in shock as she gasped.

"Wait, what?"

Chapter 37

Whittle was interrupted by several loud, garbled alarms. They blared for a moment, then died, as if their power simply faded.

"What the hell was that?" Jace worried.

"Those were the base alarms." Whittle replied. "They've never done that before."

Lights began flickering on all over the mountain range. Ash could be heard screaming in the distance, getting closer as she cried out.

"GUYS, RUN! GET AWAY FROM THE BASE NOW!"

As everyone perked up and got ready to run, Trixie came squealing happily through the tree tops over them.

"I DID IT, COME ON!"

As they looked around in confusion, They could hear Trixie talking to Ash in the near distance.

"TRIXIE WHERE YOU GOING, THE BASE IS ABOUT TO BLOW!"

"I shorted the system, come on before it resets!"

RX got on all fours.

"We should go."

Miranda and Jace climbed on, as Whittle stomped out the fire.

As they cought up just outside the forest, Ash was still yelling at Trixie.

"HOW TRIXIE?!"

"The junction core is offline," She started. "We have to go Ash, before the system resets!"

RX slid to a halt beside them.

"What's going on?" Whittle asked.

Ash took a breath.

"I rigged the base to blow! There's..."

"The bombs are offline!" Trixie interrupted. "I disconnected all the junctions from the E-1. NOW LET'S MOVE!"

Before she could say anything, Trixie wrapped her tail around Ash, and planted her on her saddle as she took off.

RX looked to Whittle.

"Follow them, genius!" She quipped.

RX quickly galloped after them.

As they rode along the mountain range, the wreckage of the Pegasus came into view, the hangar door was now fully open.

"Trixie!" Ash began. "You better start explaining this!"

"I will inside." She replied.

As they got close, Trixie hopped in to a drift, sliding into the hangar, screaching across the metallic floor.

"Told you Ash!" Trixie teased. "Guys watch the..., GUYS!?"

RX galloped as fast as she. As the wreckage came into view, The door began closing.

"RX COME ON!" Whittle cheered. "PUMP THOSE LEGS YOU SEXY BITCH!"

Trixie and Ash peeked their heads from the hangar.

"HURRY THE FUCK UP!" Ash screamed.

Turrets began firing as they locked on.

"SON OF A BITCH!" Whittle shouted. "RX FUCKING RUN!"

"Trixie!" Ash commanded. "Get to the to hangar terminal, disable the turrets. I'll hold the door."

As the door dropped lower, Ash unloaded several shots into the railing, melting the guide rollers. The door shuttered and began slowing down.

"Shit, this is sooner than I thought." Trixie muttered to herself.

Screaching to the terminal, she began typing away as fast as she could.

Plasma bolts and lazers bounced off pieces of the ship, as RX neared the door. The door creaked as the rollers busted, sending it into a freefall.

"RUN DAMNIT, RUN!" Ash and Whittle screamed in unison.

As the door approached the bottom, RX launched herself through, tackling Ash across the hangar floor as it crashed down behind them. Tumbling through a stack of crates and a pile of scrap, They all came sliding to a stop near the inner wall, panting heavily.

"Hey..., Ash." Miranda panted. "How about that drink?"

Ash groaned and dropped her head.

"Make it a triple."

Chapter 38

After making their way through the base, they stepped into the galley and took a seat at the drink bar.

After a few shots, and some chatting, Trixie slammed her bottle on the counter, giggling.

"Okay." Miranda started. "Let me get straight, You snuck in through a ventilation shaft, by turning into a smaller version of yourself? What did you call it, Puppy mode?"

"Yeah!" Trixie snorted. "Watch this."

Her suspension and tires shrunk into her frame, as her eyes went dark. Her saddle began scrunching, as her tendrils retracted into her body work. Seconds later, a hatch behind her saddle popped open, as a smaller version jumped out.

"Puppy mode!" She exclaimed.

Her voice was now a higher pitch, and her tail was replaced with a thin, clawed tentacle. Her handle bars were replaced with floppy metallic fabric, resemmbling puppy ears.

"Pretty cool, huh?" She continued.

"Did you just give birth to yourself!?" Miranda slurred.

"How come you never did that for me?" Jace wondered.

Everyone burst out laughing again, pouring themselves another round.

After downing her shot, Miranda placed her palms on her temples and giggled nervously.

"Is she gonna be okay?" Ash worried.

Whittle downed her drink with a chortle, slamming the glass on the counter.

"Miranda here is our biggest fan, Ash." She started. "She went to the G.P.S academy in hopes of reuniting us. Now, thanks to Jace and Phlanogin..., I'd say she's got a good start."
She began pouring herself another shot.
"By the way, I didn't catch that last part, Miranda. Something about you and Delta?"
Miranda snorted as she began laughing. Stepping out of her chair to catch her breath, She slipped on a puddle of condensation. Slamming her head on the floor with a loud "Thwack", She blacked out.
Whittle rushed over, as everyone burst out laughing again.
After checking her pulse, Whittle grabbed her the floor.
"I'll take her to the medical bay. Save me a drink."
Walking through the darkend corridors, Whittle hummed to herself. After a short while, she stepped into the medical bay, as lights flickered on.
"You know." Whittle chuckled. "For a G.P.S officer, you sure as hell can't hold your liquer."
After placing her on a bed, and hooking up a monitor, Whittle stepped out as the lights faded off.
Stepping back into galley, She noticed Trixie sleeping on her own saddle. Looking over, She saw Ash passed out on the couch, with Thomas's cube in her hand, and behind the counter, Jace was curled up RX's stomach.
She sighed in annoyance.
"Thanks for saving me a drink."
After chugging the rest of her's and Trixie's drinks, she wobbled over to RX and leaned into Jace with a sigh.
"I'm drunk, whatever."
Soon after she passed out, The lights faded off, and the base went quiet for the night.
A strange aura filled the air as they slept. In a room near the core, deep below the surface, 10 pink, holographic orbs flickered into existence.

They floated and shifted together, as they exited into the lower half of the base.

After some time, The orbs made their way up to the galley. They quietly floated over the sleeping crew, until they came across Ash. Faint, garbled whispers filled the air, as Thomas's cube began to glow. "Tho...mas?"

Chapter 39

Ash woke up with jolt. In a cold sweat she looked around the room frantically. After relaxing a moment, she looked down to check on Thomas. A chill shot up her spine.

"Wake up!" She commanded. "EVERYBODY GET UP NOW!"

Trixie slid off her saddle.

"Ash what's..."

She winced as the hangover set in.

"Thomas is missing!"

"Did you check the cushions?" Trixie muttered.

Ash thought for a second.

"Trixie that's not funny. This is serious, we need to..."

A soft thump could be heard, followed by Whittle giggling. Jace groaned as he stood up behind the counter, rubbing his head. Whittle raised up next to him.

"How drunk did we get last night?" Ash wondered.

"Hey, RX!" Whittle replied. "How drunk did you get?"

RX snored in response, as Whittle looked back to Ash.

"Pretty drunk I would..."

"Whittle, Thomas is gone!" Ash interrupted.

"Calm down, Ash." She replied. "It's not like he just floated off and..."

Miranda came trudging through the door tiredly, mumbling to herself.

"Hey guys?" She yawned. "Could you tell those ball things to keep it down?"

They watched as she walked over to the kitchen area.

"Seriously, I barely got any sleep."

She began making herself breakfast.

"All that whispering is annoying."

She trudged over to the counter, with a bowl of fruits and veggies, grabbing her head with a wince.

"God, that cube still hurts my head."

They looked at eachother curiously, then back to Miranda.

"Was the cube blue?" Ash questioned.

Miranda winced again.

"Yeah, and too damn bright."

Ash looked to Whittle, then back to Miranda.

"Miranda where did you see it?"

She winced with a sigh.

"By the medical..."

Ash bolted out of the galley. Whittle sighed and ran after her.

"Hey, wait for me!" Trixie exclaimed.

As her puppy form rolled out, Jace walked over to the couch, and collapsed with a huff.

"It's way too early for this."

Chapter 40

As they sprinted throught the base, Ash berated Whittle.

"Not like he just floated off, Huh?"

"Give me a break, Ash. You were drunk too."

"Fine. Which medical room?"

"Alpha." Whittle replied.

"Alpha?" Trixie exclaimed. "Why? That's all the way down."

"Call it instinct, Trixie!" Whittle replied. "I was drunk!"

They came to a rail overlooking a deep shaft.

"It's the fastest way!" Ash yelled, diving over.

"Last one down is a loser!" Trixie screamed, jumping after her.

Whittle stopped at the railing.

"You guys are idiots." She muttered.

Grabbing a nearby tether, she took a running start and leapt over.

As they fell, Ash reached for gun. As she felt the empty holster, she screamed.

"SHIT! MY GRAPPLER!"

Whittle's forearms snagged them, as the floor approached, slowing their fall. As they lifted them back to Whittle, she huffed in annoyance.

"We installed those tethers for a very good reason!"

After reaching the bottom, they disconnected the tether and quietly paced up the hall.

They stopped near the medical room, as a garbled whisper filled the air.

Ash made a "shush" motion.

Coming up to the room, they stopped and peeked inside.

In the center of the room sat Thomas's cube. The pink orbs swirled around it, as the whispers continued.

Trixie's ears quivered.

"Hey guys." She whispered. "I think that's..."

The orbs rapidly formed a grid towards the door.

"Dumbass." Ash and Whittle quipped.

As they stepped through, the orbs tightened their formation, as the whispering grew more violent.

"What are they?" Whittle pondered.

"A rouge hologram maybe?" Ash whispered back.

"Guys, I think that's Ana." Trixie said, rolling over.

Ash and Whittle tried to grab her, but she was already out of reach.

"Ana?" She asked.

The orbs tightened even more, as the whispering became malicious.

"Ana, It's me." She continued. "Remember?"

An orb shot out and slammed her, sending her into the wall.

As Whittle and Ash started over, Trixie flicked her claw.

"Hang on guys." She assurerd them.

She rolled over again.

"Ana, relax. It's just..."

Two orbs shot out and sent her into the wall again.

"ALRIGHT, THAT'S IT!" She exclaimed.

Trixie darted over and jumped into the orbs. They caught her on a small grid and began shooting themselves at her.

"ANA YOU NEED TO CHILL!" Trixie commanded. "GUYS, GET THOMAS!"

Ash darted over and snagged the cube. As she ran off, the orbs threw Trixie at her. Thinking fast, she wrapped her tendril around Ash's shoulder, and began strobing her lights rapidly.

The orbs quickly lowered to the floor, floating in a disorganized cloud.

Trixie sighed, as she leapt off Ash.

"Yeah, that's Ana."

Chapter 41

The orbs flickered and glitched, as everyone watched in curiousity.

"You're not going to say hi?" Trixie asked playfully.

The orbs flickered even faster.

"Don't be sacred Ana, it's us." She reassured.

"Ana, what's going on?" Ash demanded.

The flickering intensified, as the orbs bubbled away.

"Ash you're scaring her." Trixie pleaded.

"Trix we need to figure out just what the hell is going on here!" She replied.

"MAAASHHEEEN!" A weak, glitchy spoke.

Everyone except Trixie took a step back, as the orbs glitched and spasmed violently.

"Ana, was that you?" Whittle asked.

The orbs danced and quivered in front of the puppy synth, as the whispering picked up again. After a moment, they began floating down the hall, followed by Trixie.

"Come on." She called out. "She wants us to follow her."

As they followed Trixie and the orbs through the hangar, and down a series of corridors, they stopped in a darkened sub-basement.

Wires and strange electronic devices hung all around the massive room.

Glancing around, they noticed bits and pieces of other technology laying haphazardly across the floor.

In the middle stood a square platform, surrounded with various projector devices bolted to the frame. 3 arms hung from the ceiling, pointing at it's center.

"Ana, create, machine." The orbs whispered.

They moved on to the center of the platform, and created a pulsing circle.

"Machine, create, Ana." They continued.

"What the hell?" Ash wondered quietly.

"You built this?" Trixie asked curiously.

"Ana, create, machine, machine, create, Ana." They repeated.

"Machine, life, gone. Ana, life, gone."

The group stood confused, as the orbs moved around the platform.

"Ana, This is amazing." Ash said. "How did you do this?"

The orbs quietly danced around each of the frame pieces, then split apart, as each orb moved to the nearest projector.

They moved inward toward the center, forming a humanoid shape, which appeared to wave. The orbs then began to quiver and flicker violently, as they lowered to the floor, seeming to fall.

After a moment, the orbs floated past the crew, and hovered over a pile of collapsed droids.

"You used the service drones to build this thing, build you...," Trixie started. "But something went wrong."

The orbs hummed assuringly.

"Power failure?" Ash pondered.

Everyone remained silent.

"Those are the projectors from the hangar." She continued. "They must've drawn too much power and tripped the cycle breaker."

"What?" Whittle quipped.

"But That doesn't make any sense." Trixie started. "There was power last night."

"The solar reserves." Ash continued. "They run on the auxillary circut. That's why."

She walked over to the nearby terminal, and began typing. Moments later, a hologram appeared above it, showing a map of the base. With a few more keystrokes, the map began showing the power layout.

Lines of red pulsed softly, showing several faults around the base.
Ash sighed.
"Could you guys take a walk and check these out?"
Whittle shrugged with a sigh and paced out.
"Fine."
Trixie rolled over.
"Ash what about..."
"Trix, I'll be fine. Just go."
As she rolled out, Ash paced over to the orbs, pulling out a hidden
blaster.
"Start talking Ana!"

Chapter 42

The orbs hummed hesitantly.

"Machine, life, gone."

"What does that mean, Ana?" Ash replied with irritation.

"Home, life, still. Machine, life, gone." The orbs whispered. "life, gone."

Ash grumbled.

"Ana, I swear..."

"Life! Gone!" The orbs repeated.

They floated over to a capaciter bank, buzzing in frustration.

Ash walked over and examined the device. She noticed a tiny square indent, it appeared to have burn residue and metal flecks all around it.

"Machine, needs, new, life!" The orbs repeated.

"Alright, I got it!" Ash replied in anger.

As she huffed, the orbs shifted around, forming into circle. They began floating closer to Ash.

She redirected her pistol to the machine on the ceiling.

"Move any closer and I destroy it." She threatened.

The orbs stopped.

"Don't play dumb. What were you doing with this tech, Ana?"

The orbs sighed, floating over to the terminal. They moved about the keyboard, dropping on each key like a finger, until scematics began to appear on the screen.

Ash looked over them. Her anger turned to curiousity, then to worry, then to abject horror.

She cowered back and tripped over herself.

"Ana, w-where did you learn this information?"

The orbs floated over her, as she crawled backwards. As she reached the wall, she braced herself and anxiously waited for the orbs to strike.
"Master, must, give, machine, life. Master, must, give, Ana, life."
Ash swallowed hard, before standing to her feet.
"A-alright. How can I give you life, Ana?"
The orbs floated back to the terminal and typed in something else.
Moments later, a folder blinked on the screen, as it opened.
Several files flashed across, each holding alien equations and blocks of foreign text. Following the files, were 2 images, that sent frigid chills up Ash's spine.
On the screen was an enlarged image of a metallic square, with a Crystaline, luminescent blue matieral filling the center, interlaid with silver circutry.
Ash looked over at the capciter, then back to the screen with a deep sigh.
"Ana, if you tell anyone else about this, I will personally destroy you.
The orbs seemed to giggle, as they began a wide orbit around Ash.
"What are you doing, Ana?" She worried. "What's so funny?"
The orbs whispered softly.
"Family, home!"

⸻ ⧘⧙ ⸻

Whittle and Trixie came walking into the galley, shortly followed by Ash.
"Guy I have good news, bad news and worse news."
Miranda and Jace perked up lazily.
"Whatever Ana built, she used most of the repair matter for the ships and base. The good news..., she's currently in shutdown mode until we can make repairs."
"And Thomas?" Trixie asked.
"He's in a holding unit." Ash started. "Until we can get full power restored, he needs to stay there."

"What about the Pegasus?" Whittle asked.

Ash sighed.

"We're either gonna have to rebuild it, or get a new ship entirely."

Trixie and Whittle sighed, as RX grumbled from behind the counter.

"The base is running on solar reserves at the moment." Ash continued.

"That should be enough for the food makers, atmosperic generators and basic comforts."

There was an odd silence.

"I'm going to take the Kacyka, and pick up some repair matter. It's going to take a few days, and I need someone to come with me."

Whittle glanced at Trixie, then quickly suffled to the other side of the counter.

"Well." She started. "The Kacyka only seats two, and these three can't survive alone."

She pointed to Miranda and Jace. RX grumbled again.

"I'll stay here and keep them alive." She continued. "Plus, Trixie is already in puppy mode."

Ash glanced at Trixie with a sigh.

"Get prepared, I'm gonna go wake Penny up."

As she walked out, Trixie rolled around the counter and rammed Whittle.

"Thanks for the sell-out, Murrcooni!" She exclaimed.

Whittle picked her up, as she struggled.

"Trixie, listen." She started. "I would much rather die in space, then ride with Penny. She's a vapid bitch, and I hate her."

After she set her down, Trixie sped out grumbling.

"This is bullshit!"

━━━╫╫╫━━━

A feminine voice yawned, as lights flickered around the cockpit.

"Hey Ash!" She yawned again. "How was the show?"

Ash sighed.

"It was amazing, Penny. You didn't see it?"

"No." She pouted. "I fell asleep again."

Trixie could be heard rolling up the cat-walk. After a moment, she climbed into the cockpit with a huff.

"Ready." She sighed.

"PUPPY TRIXIE!" Penny gasped.

A small pair of mechanical arms unfolded from the ceiling, and started petting Trixie.

"Penny come on!" She protested.

"We need to make a supply run Penny." Ash started. "Mind helping us out? I'll record the show for you this time."

"Absolutley!" Penny gasped.

As the Kacyka disconected from it's gantry, A sudden realization came over Ash.

"Hey Penny why don't you relax a minute. I'll get us into space while you play with Trix!"

"OH BOY!" She squealed.

After getting the door lifted high enough, Ash darted the shuttle out and took off into the sky, as Trixie protested angrily.

"Enough Penny!" She shouted. "Can you go back to sleep for a minute? I need to talk to Ash!"

The mechanical arms folded back as Penny sighed deep.

"Ohh, okay."

After making sure she was asleep, Trixie relaxed with a few huffs.

"So where are we going Ash?" Trixie demanded.

She looked out the window and sighed.

"We're going see an old friend." Ash replied.

The shuttle flew into the stars with renewed vigor.

E^{ND!}